Emma,

Hope to
Enjoy it! Sue

Love

MW01135248

Feathers in the Blood

Susan Hankinson

authorHOUSE®

AuthorHouse™
1663 Liberty Drive
Bloomington, IN 47403
www.authorhouse.com
Phone: 1-800-839-8640

First published by AuthorHouse   3/9/2010

ISBN: 978-1-4490-7567-5 (e)
ISBN: 978-1-4490-7566-8 (sc)

Library of Congress Control Number: 2010902176

Printed in the United States of America
Bloomington, Indiana

This book is printed on acid-free paper.

If you enjoy this book you may enjoy another book by Susan Hankinson

Aunt Daisy Knows

This book is dedicated to my oldest daughter, Lori, for all the time and effort she has put into public relations for my stories, making suggestions along the way and for her belief in me.

Chapter 1

The sun was beaming brightly through the tree that was rooted directly outside CJ and Lynn's bedroom window. It was a beautiful, late summer morning, and everything and everyone was going to enjoy this day. It held promises of picnics, walks, swimming and vacations. Yes, CJ thought to himself as he lay in bed looking out the window, as soon as Lynn wakes up we'll get started on our yearly trip back to the old homestead in the mountains of Tennessee.

CJ closed his eyes and let his mind run freely, remembering all the times he and his family had visited his Dad's parents at their home in Tennessee. He had spent many summers and many school vacations there. He loved that area and he especially

1

loved the people who lived back in the mountains. They were real, down to earth folks who worked hard at their trades and showed great pride in what they could do, without electrical tools and gadgets. They only needed to be taught a skill from the head craftsman of the family and they would hone that skill until it was a perfect specimen of their ability and knowledge.

CJ got so lost in his thoughts that he drifted back to sleep, where he resumed mentally reliving parts of his childhood on the mountain. His thoughts were interrupted by the sound of someone calling to him from far away. His mind returned him to present day as he awoke to the sound of cars and people outside the window. He was glad to be awakened because he was late getting the luggage in the car. He was also at a point in his dream that rekindled the sadness and fear that he had sometimes dealt with when he was a kid visiting his grandpa and grandma back in Serpentine Gulch, Tennessee.

As Lynn heard CJ moving around upstairs, she thought it was the perfect opportunity to tease him for sleeping in. She called from the bottom of the stairs, "Claude John, it's about time you rolled out of the sack. Do you think you're on vacation or something?"

He did not reply, he just smiled to himself and finished dressing. Claude John was the way he was addressed when he was in Serpentine Gulch. Everyone was called by their birth name, first and middle. CJ never understood why, but he thought it was because there were so many relatives in a family that using both names avoided any possibility of misunderstanding of who was being spoken to or about, especially if you were talking about someone who had lived generations ago.

Just as CJ cleared the last step and entered into the living room from upstairs, Lynn handed him his traveler's mug full of fresh coffee.

"This is great," CJ said, "but first I've got to get the luggage into the car, and the groceries you bought for our week's stay."

"Well, you can forget about those jobs. I finished loading the car, making the coffee, and even paid some bills online while you got your beauty sleep. I'm really not picking on you, CJ, I know you must have been tired if you could oversleep on the first day of your vacation."

CJ could not understand why he overslept either, but he had and that was that.

"So let's go Lynn, we've got a few hours of driving ahead of us before night fall."

Although CJ knew the way to the old homestead like the back of his hand, he'd still like to be there before darkness rolled in. There were things that had to be done before he or Lynn could relax and have a bite to eat. Wood must be brought in, the house needed a little airing out, fresh oil would have to be put in the lamps, clean sheets for the bed, luggage to be taken in and most important, the little house out back would have to be freshened up and limed down. The more he thought about the chores ahead of them, the more he wondered why they looked forward to this trip each year.

As he slid behind the steering wheel of his SUV, he was once again thankful for the beauty of the day and the promise of the cool mountain breezes that were awaiting them at Serpentine Gulch. Where could Lynn be, she was pushing him to get started and now here he was sitting in the SUV waiting for her. He blew the horn with two short toots, but still no Lynn. He could not imagine what he had forgotten to get or do. He'd have to go inside and see what the hold up was. As CJ entered the front door he could hear Lynn talking on the phone. Their eyes met and Lynn spoke saying, "CJ just walked into the house. Here, Mom, speak to him yourself. Honey, it's your Mom, it's a good thing I answered the phone."

"What's wrong with Mom and Dad?" he asked Lynn as he walked over to the desk and took the phone from her hand.

"Nothing, just talk to Mom."

"Hi, Mom, what's up?"

CJ's mom, Sadie, answered him by saying that she and Dad had received a plain brown envelope from Serpentine Gulch, Tenn. addressed to him. Who would be sending him personal mail from there? He could understand mail from the municipality with a tax receipt in it or even a realtor hoping to buy the house and property for a future housing development. After all, he now owned the homestead and 55 acres of solitude.

"Mom, who is it from? We're on our way there now to enjoy some rest and relaxation. Please open the letter and see who's looking for me and why."

"Well, it seems to be from old Mr. Bowers, old Sheridan Ray Bowers who lives up on Raven Hill. He's the one who had a son named Billy Rob that you played with when you were visiting your grandparents years ago. Do you remember him, CJ?"

With a tear building in his eye CJ answered, "Yes, Mom, I remember him and his family. Billy Rob was like a brother to me then."

"Well, it seems that old man Bowers is very sick. He says he does not have much time left and he's just got to see you before he joins the rest of his family at Bowers' Peaceful Acre. He is asking you to please come see him as soon as possible. He's still at home and he must talk to you. He says he and the family always thought of you as kin and kin help kin. He don't want money, he wants your time. He's the last living member of the family. It says, 'Please come soon, very soon. Respectfully, Sheridan Ray Bowers.'"

CJ assured his mom he would find out what it was all about. He thanked her for passing on the request from Raven Hill and he also sent his love to his dad and her before hanging up the phone and heading out the door to meet Lynn in the car. They were surely late now and it would be early evening before they would see Serpentine Gulch and his childhood play ground.

As much as he loved his time there with family and friends, not all his memories were fond ones. Some were down right puzzling, scary and sad. For a day that showed great promise and good planning of a much wanted and needed vacation it seemed like everything was out of sorts. CJ and Lynn talked as they drove, about the colors of the flowers along the roadway, the traffic, and how the day had plans of its own. No matter what they remarked on, the subject always returned to Mr. Bowers and what he wanted of CJ.

By the time they where pulling into Serpentine Gulch the sun was setting and the moon was on its way up. There was no one to be seen walking along the road. Houses were few and far between, meaning that through the trees they could occasionally see a light in a window far off. The residents of Serpentine Gulch were settling in for the night.

CJ pulled into his driveway and the lights from the car shone on the front of the house. He continued around to the back and took a long, deep breath before opening the car door and heading toward the house. Lynn called out to remind him of all the things they should do. CJ would be happy just to have oil in the lamps, sheets on the bed and a bite to eat. Lynn was of a different mind. She wanted to totally prepare the house for their stay before they went to bed. She scurried about helping CJ bring in the load from the car. Neither one of them could believe that they had packed so many provisions.

The path from car to house seemed to get longer with each trip, but the truth was they were winding down from the stress of the day and the length of the trip. CJ's next endeavor was to find and clean the oil lamps that were always stored under the sink. Lynn started toward the master bedroom with fresh sheets for the bed. It had been a little bit of a struggle to make the bed while holding on to a flashlight, but not impossible - after all, she was woman. Just as she was slipping on the last pillowcase, a golden glow shone throughout the room. CJ placed the lamp on the dresser by the door and then went back to putting canned goods away.

The light from the oil lamps seem to make the old house come alive. It was so inviting and so warm for both of them as they continued to work, getting snuggled in for a week of solitude and rejuvenation. CJ emptied a bottle of water into a clean tea kettle to make some hot chocolate while Lynn was making a couple of hearty ham and cheese sandwiches to go with the veggie soup that was simmering on the stove. It was a good thing CJ had always made it a point to leave wood behind, and it was an even better choice to light the stove as soon as they got there. He knew it would be their only source of heat while in the mountains.

The kitchen was full of warm light and great smells of supper. The two filled their bowls and cups. Between the soup and sandwich and hot cocoa, and the events of the day, Lynn and CJ never made it to bed. They had decided to sit on the sofa to talk after supper so they could finish their cups of chocolate and relax before bed.

Chapter Two

As the sunshine beamed through the kitchen window, Lynn and CJ could be found cuddled up in each others arms, far away in dreamland. It was now the crack of dawn in the mountains and no resident of Serpentine Gulch would be caught sleeping after the sun made its debut. As soon as there was enough sun light to see through the trees, CJ's closest neighbor came calling to check out the car in the driveway and to chase out any squatters who might take up claim on the property.

Lynn and CJ were starting to stir from sleep. Maybe it was the sound of the dogs howling through the woods that shook them from sleep, or maybe it was the sore muscles in their bodies from the positions they slept in all night. Whichever it was, their sense to awaken was being tried and this gave way to open eyes and the sound of the dogs howling through the woods.

CJ looked at Lynn and said, "It's going to take a week for us to get off this sofa."

Neither one of them could believe that they slept all night sitting up. They laughed and moaned in unison while getting off the couch. Lynn quickly extinguished the lamp on the table and CJ looked out the window.

"Looks like Donnie Joe is on his way down the mountain trail to find out who's here. They are really great neighbors, they are always watching over the property and the house. We never have to worry when we're not here," said Lynn.

"We never have to worry when we are here," added CJ.

Donnie Joe didn't wait to be asked in. He threw open the door and entered with gun in hand. Upon seeing CJ he put the safety back into position on his gun and crossed the floor without haste to embrace his old friend. After a hug and a couple of back slaps Donnie took time to say hello to Lynn. CJ told

Donnie he saw him coming through the woods to check the house out.

"Yeah, that was me," agreed Donnie. "I thought I saw lights going into your drive last night. Pa and I decided not to disturb whoever it was, we just went down to the road and put up the road block so no one could get back out."

Lynn asked Donnie if anyone could remove the road block after he and his pa had gone to bed.

"Well, they could try. We also left the dogs out all night and the dogs don't take a strong liking to strangers. The commotion would surely wake Pa and me and that would be it."

Lynn didn't press him on it. CJ had always said some things are best not known when it came to mountain ways. Lynn decided to leave the guys alone to talk, while she made some coffee and breakfast for all of them.

When CJ was sure that Lynn had left the room, he asked Donnie Joe about Mr. Bowers. Donnie was slow to answer so CJ told him that he knew old Mr. Bowers was not well. Donnie looked at the floor for a second and then said that he and his father had gone to see Bowers just a day ago and he was in a pitiful state of health. He said he was waiting for someone special to show up and he hoped it was soon, 'cause his time was running out and there was things that had to take place for him to pass on with peace filling him. CJ was fishing for more insight when he asked Donnie Joe if he or his Pa knew who Bowers was waiting for.

"No, no, I can't say we do. He was real closed mouth about that, but in time some stranger will show up and then the whole mountain population will know."

Donnie also said that he thought old man Bowers might be a little touched in the head since his last son died from that freak accident.

"I remember that night because it was a powerful rain storm. The wind was howling and the lightning was flashing like it was day time. His son Max had just left the saw mill when he was struck down by a bolt of lightning. All the men of that clan wore necklaces with small metal tree charms around their necks and that's where the bolt hit him. It branded a picture of the oak tree in his neck.

"The mountain people gathered up on the Bowers place to give a proper burial to Max. We all prayed and sang songs of Holy passing and then carried Max up to the family burial plot to rest for eternity. That's the only time anyone but family are allowed to visit their family's resting area.

"It was said that Mrs. Bowers pined away after the loss of the last child. The old man came to town one day to get some items at the store and when he was asked about his wife's grieving, he said she grieved no more. He laid her down by Max about a week later. Bowers has been on his own for a long time," said Donnie. "The old man is real careful about who comes and goes on his property, and he's even more careful about who he speaks to."

As the men spoke about Sheridan Bowers, Lynn had placed coffee and food in front of them and then she retreated just inside the bedroom door so she could hear the conversation, but not be a deterrent to Donnie's speaking about Mr. Bowers. Lynn did not understand why CJ did not tell Donnie it was he that Sheridan Bowers wanted to see. He must have had a reason, after all, he understood the mind of a mountain man, so she thought it best not to interject.

The more Donnie spoke, the more the chills rushed through her. She loved the woods and the mountains, and she adored CJ and their life together, but the homestead and the locals always brought a feeling of uneasiness to her. She knew today he would be going to see old man Bowers and that she would not be allowed to go with him. No one would. This thought made the hair on the back of her neck stand up.

Once CJ hiked over the rim of the mountain he would be in Bowers territory. It would be no turning back for him until he was able to see and speak with Sheridan Bowers. Lynn knew that the request for CJ to meet with him had raised a lot of trepidation and maybe even a little fear for CJ. She also knew that whatever was asked of him must be very important and very guarded and time was running out fast for Mr. Bowers. But what was ahead for CJ no one could have ever seen or imagined.

Donnie had said his farewells for the day and CJ was filling his canteen and packing some food for his hike to see Mr. Bowers. Lynn watched as he pulled on his boots and strapped on his knife.

"Isn't it possible I could go with you, CJ?" asked Lynn.

"I wish you could, but that's not the way things are done around here. I'll be fine, I know these woods like the back of my hand. I'm not sure what I'll find when I get there or what will be asked of me. If you have any problem at all blow the car horn and Donnie or his Pa will be here in no time to help you."

"How long do you think you'll be gone?"

"At least till tomorrow night. It's quite a hike and that's really the best way to get there from here. I really don't think I want to try taking the SUV up the old roadway. It was a hard trip years ago with a pick-up truck and the road can't have gotten any better. The sooner I start, the sooner I'll return. Please don't worry, Lynn. Rest and read. I'll be back to drive you crazy in no time."

She walked him to the door of the old homestead where they embraced and kissed.

"Hurry back and be careful, CJ, I worry about you and I miss you, especially at night."

"I'll be fine honey, and I know the neighbors will watch after you, just as if I were here. Please tell no one where I went until I get back and we talk over what was asked of me."

CJ picked up his shotgun and headed up the hill and through the woods. Lynn watched until he was out of sight, then set about to finish cleaning up the place and scrubbing down the out house. When CJ got back things would be fresh and clean for the rest of his vacation. Lynn thought that by staying busy all day she would be able to fall asleep quickly tonight and awaken to CJ returning. He had only been gone for 15 minutes and she was worried and missing him already. Her mind raced through all the possible things that could happen to him in the woods and also on what he was going to find once he reached old man Bowers' cabin.

While Lynn kept herself busy cleaning, CJ was still hiking up the mountain on his way to the Bowers place. He, too, had thoughts racing through his mind about Lynn being left behind. He knew she would be watched over by Donnie and his Dad. He also knew she would be fretting about his hike up the mountain and what he would see and learn when he reached his destination. He was very concerned that even though he had hurried to Serpentine Gulch and on to Raven Hill that he may still be too late.

As he walked through the trees he let his thoughts take him back to his childhood adventures and friends. The Bowers clan was a tight knit group of people. They were all related to one another and they all were carpenters. Each had learned the trade from the one before. They didn't socialize much except for church on Sundays and an occasional trip to town to purchase supplies and pick up their mail.

That family was pretty self-sufficient. They had their own acreage of trees they drew from and they always replanted what they chopped down. They took care of the land and the trees so it would take care of them and their generations to come. No one knew how long the Bowers clan had lived up on Raven Hill but they would tell you it was forever. Yep, it was theirs and they claimed they paid greatly to live and eke out a living on that mountain.

Walking through these woods on a day much like today was the way CJ had met Billy Joe Bowers. He was the youngest of the clan and about the same age as CJ was at the time, around ten. It was a late summer day and Billy Joe was planting small seedlings, just as his father had told him to do. CJ had not realized just how far he had walked that day when he came upon Billy Joe, who was fully aware of CJ's approach. Billy stopped planting and said to CJ, "Hey kid, you're on Bowers property. You're trespassing and you could get yourself shot dead."

CJ's eyes grew to the size of saucers as he stammered out a reply. "My name is Claude John and I'm spending the rest of the summer with my grandparents, the Rolleys, down in the valley. I didn't mean to trespass on your property. I looked for the trees with the red paint on them so I would know if I wandered too far off the path, but I didn't see any."

"Nobody just wanders into Bowers territory and wanders back out, that's the law of the mountain."

"What are you going to do to me?"

"Well, if you help me plant these young trees maybe nothing," said Billy.

"Oh, I'll help you, no problem," said CJ.

The boys spent the rest of the afternoon putting the seedlings into the fertile earth.

"Why are we planting these trees?" asked CJ.

"Because we have to re-supply the land. The trees you said you were looking for we chopped down several days ago so my grandfather, father and brother can make beautiful furniture to be sold in the big city. That's how we make a living in these hills. Pa says if you don't put back what you take, the following generations won't be able to carve out a living. Do you get that joke, city boy? Carve out a living."

"Yeah, I get it," said CJ. "Now that all the trees are planted and watered can I go home?"

"Well, I guess you can if you want to."

CJ started to turn and walk away when Billy Joe called to him.

"Hey, CJ, would you like to see how the trees are turned into some down right beautiful furniture?"

"I sure would, but do you think your family will be alright with a stranger showing up on their property?"

"Well, we know each other pretty well now. After all, you helped plant Bowers trees all afternoon, so I reckon that will count for some friendly visiting and maybe Ma will even let us have some cool lemonade."

CJ helped Billy Rob carry the planting tools and bucket back to the Bowers domain. They talked about everything on the way to Billy Rob's home. It was mostly the difference in city people and hill folks, and the difference was great. As much as they differed in their life styles, they still grew to be the best of friends. Those differences seemed to seal their relationship together.

Once they cleared the ridge of the mountain there was the Bowers homestead with all the small outbuildings used to house the animals that sustained their existence on the mountain. They had just about everything that a person would need. Other than going to church, their trips to town were few and far between. When they did go for other reasons, it was usually only the men who would make the trip. They would have a list of provisions neatly written on a piece of paper and they would take an old pick-up truck with the words "Bowers Furniture" painted on the side. They would load that truck with sugar, flour, and other staples that they could not grow. They would also get fruits and grains, whatever it would take to restock their larder for several months. They would pay their bill in cash and not be seen again until Sunday rolled around and then they would all go to town to attend church.

They would acknowledge each parishioner and then they would quietly be seated in the same section of pews all the Bowers had sat in since the church was erected. No one ever remarked on their selection of seating arrangements and no one ever sat in the Bowers section either; after all it was the Bowers who had built the church.

CJ and Billy Rob would play and work together every time CJ went to Serpentine Gulch to visit his grandparents. Their relationship was more like brothers than friends, and because of this strong bond between them, Billy Rob's family received and accepted CJ as one of them. This was a wonderful situation for CJ's family as they truly cared about Billy Rob, too. In addition, the families were at peace with each other through their boys, so when CJ was at the Bowers homestead his grandparents never had to worry about his safety, because no one messed with the Bowers.

The sun was starting to look for it resting place on the horizon as CJ cleared the top of the ridge. It had been years since he made that climb and time and age were slowing factors in his hike. He no longer had the stamina of his youth, and he had made a few wrong turns and that had cost him in daylight. Finally, there it was, the old Bowers mountain top dwelling. CJ loved this place when he was young, but now he could feel the goose bumps crawling all over his body.

The homestead was in disrepair, its outbuildings in various stages of collapse. The mill that had run day after day cutting wood for furniture was stopped and the stream of water that turned the saw was rerouted around the mill and down the mountain. The water flowed aimlessly and without purpose. The animals were gone. The place was eerie and foreboding with all sounds of production ceased.

CJ knew he could not turn around now. In his heart he would always be welcomed here, but in his mind, he was overcome by waves of uneasiness and fear. He told himself to grow up, it's just like him, the place has aged and changed. There were no longer any Bowers to work the land. Old Sheridan Ray did the best he could until he just could not fight off the inevitable process of aging.

The sun was nesting in the western sky, and CJ was able to see a dim light in the kitchen window. He hurried his pace toward the house. Afraid to go in and afraid to stay out, especially with night falling, he lessened the distance between him and the house. As he did he caught sight of something out of the corner of his eye and stopped to see what it was. It was the sign marking the entrance to the

Bowers final resting area. It read as it did years ago and for some unknown reason the ravens still used the family plot tree for their resting spot. Funny how they have always settled on a just few branches and they seem to huddle together in that one area.

CJ continued to read the sign marking the entrance of the cemetery.

WE WORK IN WOOD, AS WE SHOULD.
WE FEED THE LAND, 'CAUSE WE CAN.
WE SOW AND WE GROW

He never really quite understood the verse over the cemetery then and it still made little sense to him now. But as a young lad it made him real uneasy and although many times he was going to ask the meaning of it, he thought better not to pry. He hurried to the front door of the spacious cabin and knocked hesitantly. After a series of raps on the door, a weak yet firm voice asked, "Who's there, and don't play games with me or you'll be a new mat on my porch."

"It's me Mr. Bowers, Claude John Rolley, you wrote me and asked that I come as soon as possible."

"How do I know it's you, Rolley?"

"Because I was Billy Rob's best friend and when I was little you gave me a small wooden tree necklace on a piece of leather and told me I was a member of the Bowers clan by adoption."

There was no answer, so CJ continued, "The rest of the clan wore small, metal necklaces in the shape of an oak tree, but I was not true blood so I was given a hand carved wooden one. I watched you make it for me. Do you remember now, sir?"

The voice weakly answered, "Yes, son, come in and rest yourself."

CJ pushed his thumb down on the latch that held the door closed and slowly opened the solid oak door. As it swung open with a squeak, he could see the lantern over in the far corner of the room cast its dim light throughout the neglected living area. His heart was surely making its presence known. It was doing a marathon race and his feet were not moving. As his eyes slowly adjusted to the lighting, he could see old man Bowers sitting in his old wooden rocker with his shotgun across his lap. From where CJ was standing Mr. Bowers looked like he would pass away at any moment. CJ turned to close the door and then cautiously walked closer to the image in the chair.

"Mr. Bowers, I'm glad to be here but real sorry to hear you're not feeling at all good."

After a short pause Mr. Bowers answered, "I thought you would never get here in time boy. I'm not just feeling poorly, I'm headed for Bowers cemetery. I've been sick for a long spell now, a long spell. I think I got me one of those city diseases. After all, I spent a lot of time taking our furniture to the city to sell. There I was right in the middle of all that city dirt and smell. It's taken the breath right out of my lungs."

"Why didn't you go to the doctor's as soon as you knew you had a problem?"

"I nursed myself with good mountain air, food and whiskey, but when it's your time, it's your time, boy. Old Doc Potter said that I needed to go to the city for some special doctor to treat me. Well, I didn't put any stock in his judgment and then I got to feeling real bad, bad enough that I could no longer carve furniture. I couldn't even run the saw mill any more." He paused, then said, "I could hardly stay on my feet all day and now I can barely walk to the outhouse. Yeah, the grim reaper is just waitin' for me to give up the ghost."

"What do you want of me, Mr. Bowers?" asked CJ.

"Well, when I realized how pitiful I was getting to be, I went to town and had some papers drawn up. I'm the last of the true pure Bowers clan. I sent out a search notice looking for a member that maybe I could have overlooked through the years. Like a distant cousin or maybe even a member by marriage that was still around. Nothing good came from the search. Oh, I had replies to the notice from all over God's creation, but not one could prove he or she was a true Bowers from birth or marriage."

At this point in their conversation old Sheridan started to cough and choke, until he turned blue. CJ jumped up to help him, but old Sheridan motioned to him to sit down, he was alright. Then suddenly the aged one drew a long, deep breath and stopped coughing. The blue tinge that covered his face slowly subsided leaving his wrinkled countenance a light shade of gray.

A few seconds passed and the old one said, "It's getting a little worse each day."

The end seemed real close. CJ told him to rest and he offered to get him some water.

"No time to rest and water upsets my stomach."

CJ said maybe he could find one of the long lost Bowers on the internet. CJ never gave it a thought that Sheridan probably never heard of the internet to begin with.

"No, no more looking," said Bowers. "It's too late for that and none of the people that showed up or wrote could tell me the Bowers secret. If they were kin or if they were married into the clan they would surely know the promise of the clan from decades ago."

CJ was around this family for years. He was even an honorary member of the family. He had never heard anything about any Bowers clan promise from decades ago.

Old Sheridan looked at CJ and smiled. "It's good to see you again my son. I have been up here on the mountain so long by myself that I didn't realize how lonely I have been until you walked in tonight. Everything and everyone is gone or at a stand still. Even the two old dogs I had for protection and friendship have passed away from old age. I finished the last piece of furniture last fall in memory of my sweet, departed wife, Nellie Jean. There was probably six or seven pieces of well carved furniture finished and ready for delivery to the buyers. I turned off all the machinery by rerouting the stream of water. I locked up all our tools in the bedroom down the hall and waited for Donnie Joe and his pa to come visit me and bring some goods from the little store down town.

"A few days later as I sat on the bench out by the cemetery the two of them drove up. They helped me back into the cabin where we had a little nip. Donnie made up some real good stew for me and I made a deal with his pa to deliver the last few pieces of furniture to the city. That would fulfill my promise to the stores and I could rest and maybe get well. The furniture got delivered right on time and in perfect condition, but I just got sicker and weaker by the day. Claude John, do you still whittle wood like you use to, my boy?"

"Yeah, I do. I even got a little better than that. I'm never going to be as good as any of the Bowers, but I got me some tools and some wood working machinery and I can make a fair chair or nightstand if I take my time."

Old man Bowers rolled his head back on the headrest of the rocking chair. The tears ran down his face and he just smiled contently at the response CJ gave him.

"You are truly a Bowers, Claude John, and I have a deep, fatherly affection for you."

CJ could look at Mr. Bowers and see he was totally exhausted and wasted away.

"Please, sir, let me help you to the sofa so you can rest."

CJ reached for the shot gun on Bowers' lap and Sheridan watched as CJ removed the twenty gauge and hung it back on the mantel by the other guns that had belonged to each of his sons. Each had a beautiful tree carved in the stock and the owner's name carved under the image of the tree. He counted five shotguns, one for each older son, one for Sheridan, and probably the other one was Mrs. Bowers', but the room was too dark to see for sure.

"Please don't go, Claude John. We have so much to talk about. We must talk before I pass on. Please child."

CJ assured him he would be spending the night.

"You must rest some, Mr. Bowers, and I have to admit that climb up the mountain took the spunk out of me, too."

Sheridan agreed to a short nap if CJ would promise to stay there. CJ told Bowers he was going to catch a little shut eye, too. He would stretch out on the sofa that stood on the other side of the fireplace. It was the same sofa he had slept on when he used to stay overnight as a child. He made Sheridan's sleeping area on the sofa as comfortable as possible, then helped the old man to lay down and rest his weary bones.

"I only need forty winks, Claude John, don't let me sleep long. I must tell you more. Promise me you'll stay."

A callused old wrinkled hand reached up and touched CJ's arm. He took hold of the hand kindly, maybe even lovingly, and he said, "On my honor as a Bowers I swear to be here when you wake from your nap, Pa Bowers."

That's the way CJ would have addressed Sheridan when he and Billy Joe were kids on Raven Hill. Old man Bowers smiled and nodded off to receive some much need sleep. As the old man slept CJ lit a couple of more lamps and tried to tidy up the area. It was in complete disarray and down right nasty. Mrs. Bowers would turn over in her grave if she saw her home in this condition. The longer CJ was on Raven Hill and in the presence of Pa Bowers, the more comfortable he felt, not uneasy as at first, but more like he was just totally surrounded by loving memories and loving family members. There was no fear, it was more like he was totally contented to be there. He wished the circumstances were different, but such is life.

CJ was surprised to find that there were so many canned goods on the shelves, there was even some smoked bacon hanging from one of them. Donnie Joe and his pa were really trying to help out Sheridan. CJ was sure he would find some perishables in the springhouse come morning. He wanted to be sure Pa Bowers got something to eat. From the way things looked, food had not been a priority for awhile.

CJ frequently checked on Bowers as he slept. The old man looked like he didn't have a pain or a care. He was sound asleep and somewhere in his dreams he was at peace. Occasionally Sheridan would call out to one of his family members while he dozed, It was like he was among them all and sharing good times and great love. CJ listened to the mumblings as he laid on the other sofa awaiting sleep. He had blown out the extra lamps he lit and left one burning low on the side table just in case Sheridan woke so he would be able to see that CJ was still there.

CJ was struggling to get comfortable on the sofa, when he thought he heard old Bowers speaking to him.

"I'm here, Pa Bowers, what do you need."

The old man rolled his head from side to side and said, "Rest and grow children, we are all safe and together, have no fear. Claude John has returned home."

It was but a whisper, but CJ was sure of the words spoken. Well, as ill as the old guy was, he was probably fighting fever as well as exhaustion. He did look peaceful, and he was not coughing or gasping as he was earlier. For this CJ gave thanks. Exhaustion was also taking its toll on CJ. He checked on Pa Bowers one more time and then drifted off to sleep. Sleep was rejuvenating and healing to both of their bodies.

Chapter Three

*C*J was talking to Lynn about starting their family when he was abruptly disturbed from his sleep. He heard Pa Bowers calling to him to wake up.

"Help me to the privy, Claude John. I must have slept all night without moving. I'm so stiff that I can hardly move at all."

CJ shook the dream webs from his head, and brought himself back to reality without ever hearing Lynn's answer to his question about a family.

"I'm coming Pa, just let me open my eyes and turn on my brain."

CJ sat up on the side of the sofa and collected his thoughts. Sheridan reached toward CJ with the hope that he would give him a much needed tug up. Between the two of them the old man was able to gimp to a make shift commode on the porch. That was about as far as his legs would take him. It appeared it was not the first time he couldn't make the trip to the outhouse.

Once seated, CJ helped to make him as comfortable as possible. Sheridan told him he was real ashamed of the shape he was in. He said when Donnie's pa would visit him a couple times a week he would clean up after Sheridan. Neither Donnie nor his pa ever said a word about the state of the cabin, and they never said a word about this nasty situation on the porch either.

"I guess they didn't want to embarrass me and they know if things were the other way around they could count on me and my closed mouth also."

CJ got Bowers back into the house and sitting in his beloved rocking chair.

"Now," announced CJ, "we're going to have some breakfast and some good hot coffee."

"Time is running out fast for me, Claude John. Please, let's sit and talk about when I pass."

CJ replied, "Let's both have our way, Pa. I'll cook, you talk. I'll listen, I promise."

"OK, then," said Sheridan. "There has been a Bowers on this mountain for at least 200 years. At least that's about as far back as was deciphered. It didn't always look like this or have the capability to function as a booming furniture business as it has in the last 100 years. My father's father really was the one to make the saw mill idea workable and he had several boys who were able to learn carving and furniture building. That was the easy part. It was the Bowers before them that are the real heroes, I guess. They were chased off their homestead in Kentucky by some mean land squatters.

"The Bowers were a peaceful clan of people. They stuck to theirselves and they didn't have much to do with outsiders either. Well, there's always a rebel in every clan and unfortunately he reared his ugly head in the past. This boy was a breathing argument for whatever question was asked. He constantly caused worry to his family."

As Sheridan spoke, CJ was rustling up a fresh pot of coffee, which he served. He then slipped out to the springhouse as Sheridan sipped his coffee where he found some milk and butter left by Donnie. Returning to the kitchen to fry up some eggs to go with the bacon he'd found hanging above the stove was a cue for Sheridan to return to the story he started. CJ listened intently but could not figure its importance for now and today.

"Where was I, oh yes, this boy's name was Robert Jake. No one's ever received the name of Robert or Jake from that time on. This boy, Robert Jake, was a lazy, shiftless lad. He never would listen to his Ma or Pa. He would never help his brothers with no chores and the last thing he wanted to do was work with wood.

"He decided that he was old enough and wise enough that he could be on his own. The family begged him to change his ways and get some sense about him, but now he was going out into the world and find his fortune. Robert Jake took off on his own in search for that elusive dream of wealth and fame. He was gone probably a good month. Then one afternoon just after the chores were completed and it was close to supper time, his Ma started yelling for the men to come quick and see.

"As they came around the side of the cabin there was Robert Jake and some raven haired woman with sharp features and shining black eyes. He was gaunt and looked to be in poor health. He told of his great love for this woman he was with and how he wanted to receive his family's blessing so he could marry her.

"Well, to receive the family's blessing would mean to receive part of the homestead when his family members died off. It was quite a request from someone who never gave a drop of sweat or blood to the land they now so loved, he wouldn't even know how to make a living with his hands. This would also mean his wife would be entitled to the land as the others passed on to their glory. Something was wrong with this story.

"That night they all sat down to supper, and when Robert's Pa started grace, the raven haired woman got up and left the table. She returned after a short time to eat and drink but never did say a prayer or apologize for her absence. Now, for a whole week Robert and this woman did nothing except pressure his mother and father for the blessing. As Sunday rolled around the chores were finished early and breakfast was served early for the next few hours would belong to praise and worship. This was before the church was built in town, so all were expected to attend and gather in a small shaded area just a short distance from the newly erected barn. Benches were placed for sitting comfort and the family Bible was on the beautifully carved altar that was brought from the house each week.

"Once again Robert showed up in time for the opening prayer, but his female friend was nowhere to be found. The worship continued as it had always been. Each one attending the service was uneasy about the absence of Robert Jake's new found love. When the service ended they headed for the house for some coffee and pie to hold them over until lunch was served.

"As they entered the house, there was the mystery woman sitting at the table. She seemed to be deep in thought. Ma asked why she had not joined them for church service out under the tree. She turned her head sharply towards the older woman and after a long defiant stare, she said it was not her belief and she wanted no part of it.

"At that remark my uncle told her and Robert Jake to move on, because they wanted no part of her either. There would be no welcoming of her into their family and definitely no blessing given to either one of them. The raven haired woman cursed, ranted, and raved at the family as a whole and each member individually. Mostly what came out of her mouth sounded as though she was cursing each member and all they owned. Robert Jake rushed to her side to calm her down, but in turn she raised her arm and he fell to the floor weeping in disbelief that this could be happening.

"My uncle grabbed his gun from the mantel and waved her toward the door. He told her to leave and never darken their doorway again. The woman laughed and walked through the door and down the steps. Robert Jake had been able to compose himself enough to call out to her to wait for him. She yelled back to him, 'Don't follow me. I do not want nor love you, I never did, you fool. Before the sun goes down you will sleep under the watchful eyes of the raven forever, and your family will never forget me, ever.'

"Robert Jake was sure he could make everything right with her and his family if he could only speak with her and calm her down. He ran out the door and as he was dashing down the steps he misjudged his footing and fell forward with such force he broke his neck on impact with the ground. The family was totally devastated, and by afternoon that Sunday, Robert Jake was the first to be buried under the tree that set up on the knoll from the house. Later others would join him there as they passed from this world.

"As my uncle and the other boys were tamping down the earth over their loved one, Robert, they became aware that for some reason a large, black, raven had taken rest on one of the branches above the grave. My aunt rushed to the gravesite and placed hand-picked flowers at the base of the newly constructed cross. As she turned in grief to walk back to the house, she was sure that the bird was mocking her with its song. 'Shoo, shoo,' she called out to it. It flew up in the sky and circled around until my aunt was on the porch and then it came to rest over the grave again.

"There was very little said all day. The chores were taken care of and grief could be seen in the eyes of the family members. After supper that night my uncle made it a point to express his feelings about all that had occurred. 'Now that we have seen and lived through this heart breaking day, we must be extra careful of the choices we make in bringing others into our family. Robert Jake's name will be a curse to this family and neither of these two names shall ever be given to any member of this family, nor will any member of this family marry someone with either of these names, or they will be put out of this family never ever to be spoken of again.

" 'Faith and family are our primary concerns. We must be on guard always. I am convinced that because that man that we buried today out of greed and selfishness brought a witch into our domain who lured, then killed, our loved one when we would not open our lives and accept her ways. She cursed our son and will now send ravens to sit above his grave as a constant reminder of her anger toward the Bowers Family.'

"As my uncle spoke, the ravens came and sat in the tree branches above Robert Jake's grave. They squawked as if mocking he who was left.

"CJ, now you know why the Bowers have always been a close knit family with little outside social dealings unless it was church related."

CJ watched the uneasiness of old Sheridan as he sat on the sofa rubbing his thumb and forefinger together and staring out the window that afforded him a view of his final resting place and all the relatives that had already passed before him. It was obvious that the old man was still declining in health but his strength was holding because he was eating better, plus he could rest and relax knowing CJ was there. The two of them just sat quietly sipping their cups of coffee, until Sheridan announced Donnie and his pa were coming up the lane.

"That's a good thing," said CJ. "A little company would be good."

There was a knock on the door and in came Donnie and his pa.

"You're looking a bit stronger, Sheridan," said Donnie's pa.

CJ got the two older gents coffee and then asked Donnie if he would step outside so they could talk.

"That would be fine," said Donnie. "You can help carry in the groceries we brought you from town."

CJ told Donnie how he had to go back to his cabin today or Lynn was going to be worried sick. He was only supposed to spend one night with Pa Bowers, but he just could not leave him on his own. The man was too ill and too weak, and maybe even a little scared, although he would not admit it. Donnie thought that he and his Pa could spend the night with Bowers as long as CJ was to return so the two men could be home before nightfall the next day.

Donnie and CJ entered the house with their arms full of grocery bags. Pa Bowers had drifted off to sleep as he and his friend were talking. Donnie spoke to his father about staying the night so CJ could go home, pick up clean clothes, see Lynn, and get a doctor for Sheridan who would be better qualified to treat him.

The local doctor did his best, but he was older than time and not up on the new medical breakthroughs and medications. After all, there was very little to test his ability, or encourage him to increase his knowledge medically. The people of Serpentine Gulch were able to do their own doctoring by using plants and herbs and trust in the Almighty. He would choose if they made it or not, and that was the way life was lived in these mountains.

Donnie Joe and his father decided they could stay with Sheridan while CJ returned home for the night. Old Sheridan was still sound asleep as CJ loaded his knapsack for the trek back down the hill. The two mountain men realized that the cabin was a lot cleaner since CJ had come to visit and they continued cleaning up while Sheridan slept. CJ thanked them as he picked up his knap sack and headed for the door.

"I promise to be back by nightfall tomorrow, guys."

"We know you will, CJ. Here, Pa and I want you to take our pick up. We don't think it's smart for you to take the woods. It's too late in the day and you won't make it by sun down. These trees at night have a way of spooking a man when he's out there hiking or camping. Even us die hard mountain people don't like to mess in the woods at night. There just seems to be an uneasiness about the way the trees sing when the wind blows through them, especially when it's a full moon-like tonight."

"Wow, thanks for the scare, it works. I really appreciate you loaning me your wheels. Not because of the singing trees or the full moon, but because of my age and the distance I've got to go."

They all laughed, but with quiet reservations. Donnie tossed the truck keys to CJ as he opened the door. CJ caught the keys and continued on his way to the pickup. It was late in the afternoon. The day had seemed long and CJ found himself unnerved by all that was happening and all he was being told.

As he walked from the porch to the truck, he stared at the ravens that had come to nest in the branches of the cemetery tree. He could see they only chose the limbs that were directly above the resting place of Robert Jake. Although there was a beautiful hand carved cross with Robert's name inscribed on it that would have securely held the weight of several birds, the dark winged watchers did not approach the cross, they stayed where they always roosted, on the same branches, on the same side of the tree, since the death and burial of Robert Jake Bowers.

Dang, CJ thought, old Sheridan could really tell a folk story. At that time the ravens left the tree and circled over CJ and the truck. Several birds dived down and hit him on the head and shoulders. He opened the truck door and threw his knapsack in and followed it with alarming disbelief. Once he was inside the pick up, the birds regrouped and headed back to the cemetery. CJ's heart was pounding in his chest, his mind was replaying the incident in his head, and his level of fear was at an all time high for just a few minutes.

He started the truck and told himself that the birds must have been spooked by the gust of wind that had blown up from the mountain ridge. He hoped that no one in the house saw it happen, especially Pa Bowers. It would only give more credence to the story about Robert Jake. He knew it would, because deep down in CJ's heart, he knew the birds did not want him there. Putting the truck in gear and staring at the ravens, he started down the mountain to Lynn, a place where he could find comfort and rest.

When he was a child, he had ridden in the back of Sheridan's pickup many times and even then the road was a bumpy mess. Donnie's truck was the same age as Sheridan's was thirty years ago, so the memory of the drive down the twisting mountain trail made it possible for CJ to really relive this adventure again. He knew this would be a long 15 minute adventure that would bring him to the base of the mountain on the opposite side of town.

He watched in the rear view mirror as the sun was slowly setting on the horizon. He truly wanted to be off the trail and safe in town before night covered Serpentine Gulch. He really wanted to be back in Lynn's arms and to be able to feel the safety of his own cabin. CJ could not release the scene of the ravens attacking him. It played over and over in his head. He was glad that Donnie and his Dad were with Sheridan up there on Raven Hill.

Chapter Four

C J could see his driveway just as the sun was passing its light to the moon. There would be so much to accomplish tomorrow. This was turning out to be a wasted vacation as far as rest and relaxation. The whole situation was overwhelming and at times unbelievable. As he pulled into the drive and parked the truck, Lynn opened the door. CJ stepped out of the pick up and Lynn rushed to be at his side.

"I've been so worried about you and as the day dwindled on I wasn't sure you would make it back. I was afraid you would lose your way in the woods and I just plain missed you."

They hugged and kissed each other sharing love, security, and thankfulness that they were together again. CJ told Lynn that it was not over yet

"I'll explain inside," he said, "after I get cleaned up, and maybe you could rustle me up something to eat and drink."

"Sure," said Lynn as she headed for the kitchen.

"Great," said CJ as he headed for the bedroom to use the bathing bowl and sponge bathe.

The cabin glistened and smelled so fresh and inviting, a lot different than it was a day ago. Lynn must have worked non-stop to make everything shine. She could be a much needed and wanted asset at Bowers' cabin, but that would not be fair to her. The way they lived on Raven Hill was like entering a totally different time zone. And if evil was lurking up there as Sheridan hinted, CJ would not want to expose the love of his life to it.

He finished bathing and was buttoning up his pajamas when Lynn called him to eat. They sat at the table and for a second they exchanged a smile which said everything loving and kind their hearts were feeling. CJ wanted to tell Lynn everything that happened on Raven Hill, but he didn't want to scare her.

He explained the living conditions Sheridan was existing in. He also made it very clear that when the family was alive the cabin and out sheds were meticulously maintained. With Bowers health declining and age increasing the old guy just seemed to have all he could do taking care of himself. CJ assured Lynn that although he was truly ill he was holding his own and that CJ was going to try to get one of the medical doctors from the nearest hospital to come and see Sheridan. Maybe there would be some way of saving his life, but somehow CJ really didn't think that was what old man Bowers wanted.

Lynn listened to every word intently as they talked and ate supper. Now that supper dishes were cleared from the table and he and Lynn were enjoying a cup of hot coffee, CJ went on to tell Lynn that Donnie and his pa were kind enough to stay with Sheridan for the night and they even let him borrow their pickup truck so he could get home before darkness fell.

Lynn put her cup down and stared at CJ for a second, then she asked, "What do you mean for the night? You sound as though you are going to be returning to Raven Hill tomorrow."

"Well, not tomorrow morning. First I have to find a doctor who will see Sheridan, then do some more shopping for food and cleaning supplies."

Lynn's eyes filled with concern and tears.

"I'm so sorry things are the way they are Lynn. I know it's not fair to you. This vacation is our high point every year. I miss not being with you and I worry about you down here alone with me on the mountain. Maybe it would be best for you to pack up and return home until I can work this out or until God calls Sheridan home. No matter which way it goes I will be here for awhile."

CJ continued to rattle on with his thoughts flying out of his mouth without his being able to control it. All the events that had occurred since that phone call from his mother were overwhelming all his thoughts and feelings. Lynn said nothing; she finished her cup of coffee and went to the sink to do the supper dishes.

He watched her work at the sink, but had nothing comforting to say to her. He knew it was going to take longer than a week to handle the problems before him. He also knew he had accrued a lot of sick time at work so he could draw that time for extra vacation. He was afraid Raven Hill was going to be his home for awhile whether he liked it or not. And he liked it not.

However, he loved old man Bowers and his family members that had passed and he felt kinship to them, maybe even stronger than he felt for his own family. Why that was he didn't understand, he only knew he would see this task ahead of him finished to his best ability and Sheridan would be able to rest in peace.

Lynn finished the dishes and headed to bed with CJ following behind her. Once in bed, they spoke not, but they snuggled into each other arms for much needed rest and refuge.

Morning seemed to come quick. CJ squinted his eyes as the sun darted its morning rays into the cabin. The smell of coffee wafting from the kitchen meant that Lynn was up and making breakfast for them. He was slow in walking to the kitchen; every muscle in his body ached from being pushed for the last two days. Lynn had heard the lack of his snoring, which told her he was awake and on his way.

The table was set and the coffee was poured. CJ sipped at his coffee and looked at Lynn watching him.

"I'm sorry, honey, really I am."

"I know it's not your fault, it's just part of life and who you are."

CJ picked up his watch and panic ran though his veins. "Forget the food Lynn, it's so late. It's 10 o'clock! Why did you let me sleep so late? I've got to be back on Raven Hill no later than 4 o'clock. Donnie and his pa need time to get off the mountain before sunset. It's imperative they're gone by then."

Lynn looked at CJ with total puzzlement.

"Why must they be off the mountain by sunset?"

"Because of the birds and the trees and the animals. It doesn't matter, don't worry about it. I've got to make calls to find a doctor, now."

Lynn stepped in front of CJ as he went to get his cell phone from the bedroom. "I already hired a doctor from two towns over, he'll be here by 1 o'clock. He is going to stop at Dr. Potter's first and discuss Sheridan's case, then he will be here. I've explained he will have to travel up the mountain to Raven Hill to examine Sheridan. He'll do it and he will then advise us what would be best for Mr. Bowers."

CJ could not believe his ears. Not only had Lynn taken care of getting a doctor, she also read his mind and requested that his sick days be turned into more time off so he could take care of his loved one. The weight was lifting off CJ's shoulders ton by ton. With that taken care of breakfast was wonderfully welcomed and enjoyed.

Next was the trip to the local store for the provisions needed to sustain life on the mountain. The clutter in the cabin had been taken care of but it still truly needed to be cleaned and scrubbed. Old Ben Longer had owned Serpentine Gulch's dry goods store for as long as CJ could remember. As CJ and Lynn entered the double doors, there stood old man Longer with the same broad smile and deep set blue eyes. The shelves were sparsely stocked and the small ice box that still kept cold from lake ice had little to offer. Cleaning goods were limited to bleach, ammonia, and small boxes of borax. This was never going to do. CJ looked at Ben and Ben stared deep into CJ's face, then he spoke.

"It's you, my boy. It's truly you, CJ Rolley. As I live and breathe you are here, at least for a spell. Donnie said you are taking care of old Sheridan Bowers up on Raven Hill. Is that so boy? It's not a welcoming place anymore. With the death of each family member the place got stranger and stranger. Funny things started to happen up there, according to people who used to hike and camp that mountain. I don't think anyone has been enjoying those woods for 2 or 3 years now. It was probably old man Bowers scaring people away.

"He don't like outsiders. He's a might touched they say, since his beloved family died off. Well, never mind that, is he still alive, haven't seen him in years. Donnie and his pa won't say much about him."

"He's still kicking, said CJ. "I just wanted to stop by and say hello again."

"Did you need anything today?" asked Ben

"No, no," said CJ. "This is my wife, Lynn, and we just wanted to be sociable and call on you. We got to go but we'll be around for awhile and we'll talk again real soon."

With that said, CJ and Lynn left. They knew they would have a twenty mile trip ahead of them to the next town for the goods they needed for CJ's stay at Sheridan's cabin. The rush was on so they could be back in time to meet the doctor, plus CJ wanted to help get Lynn started back home. He was praying to have everything done before sunset on the Mountain. It would be a tall order to fill, but for everyone's safety he would have to find a way.

He could feel the uncertainty and the uneasiness building in his mind and stomach as he drove to the town of Sunnyside.

Compared to Serpentine Gulch this was like New York City but without sky scrapers or subways. The town was huge in comparison. This was one of the places where the Bowers sold their furniture. He would never come here for medical help as long as he was conscious, because he was sure this was where he got sick. Not that he was getting older or because he was not taking the best care of himself or maybe because he was depressed and alone for a long time, no he was sure it was the lack of fresh, clean mountain air and the amount of strangers he interacted with and shared air with.

Well, he thought to himself, if you really gave Sheridan's reasoning a little thought, it is possible to pick up lots of germs and diseases from others. You become immune to your family's germs, but put yourself among strangers and your immune system goes into overdrive and sometimes allows a virus bug to get through. In Sheridan Bowers' case it was probably all of the above and then some.

"There's a large grocery store, CJ," said Lynn.

"Great find, Lynn."

CJ pulled into the parking lot and looked for a space as close as possible. After 3 times around the lot hoping for a close parking space, CJ headed for the last row of unused spaces and parked his SUV in the first place he could. Time was wasting and they still had to be back to Serpentine Gulch by 1 o'clock to meet with the doctor.

He and Lynn exited the car and headed for the main door of the store. Once inside, CJ grabbed a cart and they headed for the aisles. The fact that neither one of them knew the layout of the store made the task of finding what CJ needed and wanted more time consuming and more frustrating. With the last cleaning item placed in the cart, they headed for the first check-out that had the fewest amount of people in line.

With the goods collected, paid for, and bagged, out the door they went. CJ loaded the bags of goodies into the SUV and started up the vehicle. He carefully checked to his right and left before leaving the parking space. It was then he noticed that Lynn was paler than normal and quieter than normal, also.

He had been so concerned about old man Bowers that he never realized that Lynn was not herself.

"Lynn, are you okay?"

"I've had days when I felt better, but I'll be fine. Please don't worry."

"We'd better get moving if we're going to get back in time to meet the doctor."

"We'll be fine. How about we stop and get a cup of tea or something to eat."

"If you really think we have the time, a cup of tea would be a good thing. My stomach is a little upset."

CJ pulled out on the road and stopped at the first burger place he saw. He jumped out of the SUV and got Lynn and himself a cup of tea and a burger with fries. He returned to the car to see Lynn smiling at him.

"I'm sorry, CJ, but I was fine this morning before we left the cabin and then as we drove along I felt queasy. The feeling is starting to pass now. I'll eat a little of the burger and drink my tea and I'll be fine. You can drive and eat on the way if you like. Honest, it will be fine, and thanks for putting up with me."

On the way back to Serpentine Gulch Lynn and CJ finished their food and drinks. Lynn felt better and CJ felt more in control of the situation, as far as time and getting Lynn to eat and drink something. Everything seemed to be back to status quo. They would be back to the cabin by 1 o'clock and Lynn was feeling a lot better. She never was able to handle high pressure situations without her body taking a toll from it. Whenever CJ would tease her about her inability to chill out under pressure, she would say, "It's in my genes. I come from a long line of high strung people who choose to act out their inadequacies rather than give into them. Lucky for you, CJ," she would say, "because it makes you look like a rock in troubled times."

"Yeah, we made it, Lynn, it's 12:31 and we are pulling into our driveway with 29 minutes to spare."

"I'll help you put the perishables in the ice box until it's time to go to Raven Hill," said Lynn.

"Thanks, babe, and looky, here comes our doctor, I think. Lynn, please meet him and bring him in the cabin while I carry these bags in, okay?"

"Will do," was her reply.

Lynn waited for the cobalt blue BMW to come to a stop behind their SUV before she headed toward it. The driveway was full at this point; between Donnie's pick-up, their SUV, and now the doctor's BMW, there was no room to move easily. Lynn slid between the hedge bushes and the vehicles until she reached the front of the BMW. There inside the car was a very distinguished man collecting his medical bag and some other items. He opened the driver's side door and climbed out. He looked much younger outside of the car than he did though the windshield. He asked if Lynn was Mrs. Rolley, then introduced himself as Dr. Andrew Miles.

Lynn invited him inside to meet her husband, Claude John. As they walked to the door, Lynn explained that CJ was Mr. Bowers' caretaker at this time. She added again how thankful they were that Dr. Miles had come this far out to see and treat Sheridan, especially knowing that he would still have to face the ride up the mountain. What he didn't know was that it would be done in Donnie's pick-up truck, which wasn't the tidiest vehicle.

Lynn held the door of the cabin open as Dr. Miles entered. "Hi," said CJ, "I'm Lynn's husband, CJ. Thanks so much for coming out"

"I'm Dr. Andrew Miles."

They shook hands, then CJ thanked the doctor all over again. "It's a pleasure to meet you, Dr. Miles and I truly thank you for coming out of your way to help a dear old friend of mine, Sheridan Bowers."

"Well, sometimes these old mountain people either won't or can't leave their cabins and I, too, was born and raised back in the sticks. I can appreciate how they feel about big cities and strangers."

"Is that why you became a doctor?" asked Lynn.

"Well, that's some of it, but that's enough about me. How soon can we get started on this quest?" asked the doctor.

"Just give me enough time to pack some provisions in the pick-up and we'll be on our way. I'm afraid you'll have to move your car, Dr. Miles, when we're ready to go."

"That's not a problem. I'll meet you outside, CJ"

As the doctor walked out the door Lynn followed CJ to the kitchen.

"CJ, you will be bringing the doctor back down the mountain tonight, won't you?"

"Well, probably not, Lynn. I was hoping Donnie and his dad would drop him off for me. There is no reason to return and Sheridan can't be left alone either. Why did you ask?"

"Because I was hoping to meet Sheridan and see Raven Hill before I went home. I've heard so much about him that I'm curious, well, maybe even a little nosy."

"I really don't think it's a good place for you to go to."

"Why not, CJ?"

"It's run down and very messy and Sheridan talks about strange things that took place up there."

"It's probably that he has a fever and his mind plays tricks on him."

"Think about it, Lynn, there is no way to get back down without hiking once Donnie takes his truck."

"I can't believe that our SUV can't make the hill climb."

"Please, Lynn, I would feel better if I knew you were home safe and sound."

"I would feel better if I knew you were safe and sound and not alone up there on Raven Hill, Claude John Rolley."

"I love you, Lynn, but I can't stand here and argue about this. The doctor is waiting and time is running out. Get your clothes in the SUV so we can both leave at the same time and please call me on my cell when you get home, honey."

"Fine, CJ, if that's how it has to be, then that's it."

CJ grabbed the bags of groceries and a small blanket from the sofa and started out the door towards the pick-up. He placed the bags in the back and as the doctor watched him he placed the blanket on the seat of the truck.

"Thank you," said the doctor. "That seat is a mess. Can we take my car or your SUV instead?"

"I wish we could but your car sits too low for the mountain ruts and Lynn is headed home until this crisis has passed. I've held off using the SUV to climb the mountain, because I did not want Lynn to be stranded if I got half way up and could not go any further."

Lynn was coming out the door of the homestead with her suitcases in tow. She locked the door and headed to the SUV to load in the suitcases and make the trip back home. CJ reached out and took her by the arm.

"Lynn, I love you and I am going to miss you a lot. Please take care going home and don't forget to call me as soon as you get there. By then I'm sure the doctor will have figured out what must be done to help Sheridan, okay Baby?"

I guess so, CJ. Thank you Dr. Miles and I hope you can figure out what to do with Mr. Bowers."

The doctor had moved his car and parked it along the front of the property. He and CJ climbed into the truck and backed out of the driveway. CJ and Lynn waved to each other and their hearts cried out when their minds realized that they would be apart during all this confusion. Lynn watched as the pick-up pulled forward. CJ blew the horn and he and Dr. Miles drove to the other end of town, where the climb up to Raven Hill would start.

Chapter Five

*L*ynn slowly backed the SUV out of the driveway and headed for the interstate, as CJ had expected her to do. The interstate was also on the other end of town. The closer she got to the entry ramp, the more Lynn knew how much she was going to miss CJ, especially with her back home and him up on Raven Hill. They had always faced any woes together and this would be their first time apart. Lynn was still having that uncomfortable feeling in her stomach that sickened her a few days ago.

The ramp was just ahead of her to the left, but the Raven Hill turn off was also ahead of her to the right. Right was the way she was going. She did not want to make CJ angry, she just wanted to be with him and support and love him through this ordeal.

She also knew she would feel better emotionally and physically if she could be with him. The worst that she thought could happen is that she might get stuck in one of the ruts on the mountain trail. She had no idea how much doom, gloom and chaos was connected to Raven Hill.

The anxiety mounted as Lynn took the right turn on to the secondary dirt road that would lead her up the side of the mountain. She wanted so to be with CJ and she wished it was because he wanted her to be by his side through this unsettled time. It was totally out of character for her not to be honest and compliant to his wants and needs. She was scared for Sheridan's health and very concerned about CJ and his physical and mental state. She was also concerned about her own well being. She was not feeling well these days and it was frightening. Her health had never been such an alarming thought to her. With all that was going on she knew the stress level was more that either of them had ever gone through, especially apart.

Lynn drove as she thought over all the events that had occurred since the original phone call from CJ's mother on the first day of their vacation. It was so amazing how involved with the Bowers clan CJ had become as a young child and now here he was making decisions about Sheridan's health and property. I guess you never know what can happen as you're going through your everyday life. Not all the people that enter your circle of acquaintances and friends really sever the ties between them and you. It seemed amazing how CJ never even thought about the Bowers much but Sheridan never stopped thinking about him.

"Great," she thought, "now here we are giving up our vacation and comfortable life style to cater to Old Man Bowers' needs."

Just then the front right tire hit a deep rut in the road and shook the whole SUV, including Lynn and her train of thought. "Oh my goodness, this road is terrible and it's impossible to miss the potholes. I've got to be more careful driving."

She realized that her full attention had not been on the road, it was on her anger toward Sheridan. Where this anger was coming from she was not sure of, but she just felt as though CJ was putting the Bowers' needs above his love for her. That really ate at her and her level of compassion for others.

The road was not getting any smoother, and she was probably only about half way up. The worst thing that could happen on this rough road was probably trying to pass another car. Lynn hoped she would make the top before Donnie and his father or CJ with the doctor and Sheridan had to make the trip down. At least the sun was still high in the sky and visibility was good, even with the trees overhanging the road. Lynn thought about how CJ had said how eerie it was traveling to Raven Hill. She thought it was beautiful area, untouched and so natural, it just needed a smoother road.

CJ and the doctor had already completed the long trek up the mountain and the doctor was examining Sheridan. CJ, Donnie and Donnie's father walked out on the porch to talk and give privacy to the doctor and his patient. Donnie and his father thought that Sheridan was getting weaker and was having a harder time breathing .CJ just listened and shook his head in total confusion of the situation and maybe also in his inability to change how things were.

He intently listened to what Donnie was saying as his eyes scanned up to the cemetery. Much to his surprise the ravens were gone. CJ abruptly yelled,

"Look," as he pointed toward the old oak tree in the cemetery. "Those damn birds are gone. Look, guys, they're gone. When did they leave the tree?" he asked "How did you get them to go away?"

Donnie and his father stood there looking at the tree. Donnie's pa turned back to CJ and said, "This is the first we seen them gone. They were there this morning, just sitting and watching."

Upon hearing that response CJ opened the cottage door and hurried in. He was sure if the birds were gone probably Sheridan was too. He knew he was letting this place and its circumstances get to him, but his reaction to all that was going on was out of his control. The doctor stopped CJ from speaking out by putting his finger to his mouth, the universal sign for quiet.

"Shhh." said the doctor, as he escorted CJ back out to the porch. "I've finished examining Mr. Bowers, and I believe he is suffering from pneumonia and severe dehydration. In addition, he's generally just old and terribly run down. It's amazing he is still alive. I've started him on an I.V. with antibiotics, but he needs more than that if he's ever going to make it. He's really in bad shape and it looks like he's been in this condition for quite awhile. The bottom line is that he is a mountain man and that's the way he chose to live. Until he reached this point in his health no one would be able to get him medical help."

With that being said, the doctor reached into his pocket, took out his cell phone, and called for an air lift evacuation unit to be sent to Raven Hill for the purpose of emergency transport to University Central Hospital. He ordered a bed in the IC unit and around the clock nurses for Sheridan Bowers.

As the doctor continued to order tests for Sheridan, the three men stood looking at each other, each feeling relief from the responsibility and fear of taking care of this mountain legend. They all knew the hospital was where he needed to be.

Lynn had no idea what was occurring up on Raven Hill, but she could hear the sound of the helicopter props. She did not make the connection until she topped the hill and saw the medivac landing in a semi-open area above what looked like a cemetery. She pulled the SUV over and watched as everyone there helped to move a person into the helicopter along with the doctor and the medical staff.

She knew two things, one, it had to be Sheridan and two, he was still alive. The number three entered her mind with the attached thought; it's too bad that they don't just let him pass on, after all he's old, sick, and upsetting everyone else's life. He had lived his time and he probably doesn't care to continue down life's road anymore, anyhow. Lynn regained control of her wandering mind and could not believe that she had even entertained such a cold, uncaring thought. If this was happening to an old, sick animal, she would be the last one to give up on it and let it die or put it down. Why was she so heartless in her thinking?

As the helicopter lifted, CJ caught sight of the SUV and Lynn. At first he was furious that she deceived him and made the trip up the mountain in the SUV, but then he ached to hold her and feel her love and strength. He half ran to the SUV and when Lynn saw him coming toward her she turned off the vehicle and opened the door to greet him. She hoped he wasn't too angry with her. She needed to be by his side and the trip up the hill was exhausting. Her stomach was in knots and her thoughts were running in areas her compassionate heart did not want to go.

CJ helped her out of the SUV and she embraced him and softly spoke in his ear. "Please, CJ, don't be angry with me. I need to be with you. I love you, you're my soul mate."

CJ held her and he could feel how exhausted she was as he kissed her neck, hoping to calm her thoughts. She trembled in his arms with relief and with a dark sense of foreboding.

"What happened," she asked as she broke the embrace they were sharing.

"Dr. Miles had Sheridan flown to University Central Hospital, he's in real poor health. The doctor's medical opinion was he was suffering from acute pneumonia and severe dehydration, maybe more. They won't know until the tests are all done, but it does not look good. The doctor could only promise the best health care would be given, the rest is up to Sheridan."

CJ had tears in his eyes as he spoke, and Lynn had anger in her thoughts as she watched the worry and concern draw lines across his brow. Donnie and his pa had unloaded the provisions from their pick-up truck and placed them in the cabin. Not being sure what CJ was going to do at this time, they drove up by the SUV and asked if he had need of them. CJ looked over the truck to the old oak tree as he tried to collect his thoughts.

"No, I think all that could be done was done."

He thanked them both for their help and for the use of the truck. He could see that the day was winding down fast and the night shadows once again were creeping up the hillside.

"Well," said Donnie, "me and Pa are going back down the mountain before night falls and it would probably be a good idea if you and your Mrs. either followed us or got inside for the night."

Donnie was careful not to rekindle any fearful thoughts for CJ and also not to spark any for Lynn. CJ was more than ready to leave Raven Hill. He took Lynn by the arm to help her back into the SUV but she did not budge.

"Please, CJ, could we please just spend the night here and leave in the morning. I really feel sick to my stomach and I am not looking forward to making the return ride tonight. We have food and water and you really wanted to clean up the cabin. I would really like to just relax and have a bite to eat and settle my stomach down before we hit that cattle trail again."

CJ did not want to stay there, but he did not want to worry Lynn either over his childish fears that really seemed stupid now. After all, the birds were gone and Sheridan was receiving the medical help he needed. There was really no reason why they could not spend the night. They would get some dinner and rest. Tomorrow they would clean up the cabin some and still be back at their old homestead by night fall. They were not cut off from society. They both had cell phones, the doctor had CJ's phone number and Donnie and his father knew where they were.

CJ looked at Lynn and said that maybe it would be best if they stayed the night so she could rest. Hopefully she would feel better in the morning. Donnie and his pa looked at each other on hearing this and then both looked at CJ with uneasiness written across their faces.

"Mrs.," said Donnie, "that cabin is real messy inside, not a place where you could find much comfort. The old man was not real good at cleaning and then he got too sick to do much. It's a place where memories, time, and solitude are your only company. You sure you want to stay here tonight? Make up your mind because the sun is going down fast and the mountain has its own way of celebrating at the end of the day."

"I'm sure I want to stay," said Lynn, looking at the men in the truck, "after all, I've heard so much about this place that in the morning I hope to see it all and take a walk around the out buildings."

If Lynn had glanced at CJ upon making that statement she would have seen the battle going on inside of him, the one that was totally in love with this mountain when he was a kid and the one that was totally uncertain about the power of a curse made decades ago.

Donnie said, "CJ, we got to go, you understand?"

"Yeah, go," answered CJ, "we got our phones and Lynn's probably got a little stomach virus. We'll be fine. Things seem to be more normal now. Bye, and thanks again."

"Do you want us to come back tomorrow and check up on you two?"

"No, we can call out if we need anything. And we got good wheels to get back down and a good spare tire in the back of the SUV."

"Okay, then, we'll see you."

Donnie's dad drove very slowly giving CJ and Lynn time to get to the cabin. Donnie watched out the small back truck window as his pa drove on, and Pa was looking into the side mirror, both of them staring at the old oak tree in the cemetery. They were trying to figure out where those taunting birds had gone and why. With CJ and Lynn inside the cabin Donnie's pa turned on his head lights and picked up speed. Night was coming and the mountain was taking on a new look. Donnie and his father wanted off this mountain before the bright sheer curtain of day was replaced by the black drape of night.

Once inside Lynn stood still as CJ lit a couple of old kerosene lamps. It truly was in need of some TLC and a lot of airing out. CJ had been going on with a rambling explanation as to the messy state of the cabin from the time he and Lynn walked in, but Lynn had not heard a single word he said. She was too busy just looking and feeling. The smells of kerosene, wood ashes, age and dampness seemed to wrap its presence into a bouquet of excitement, peace, romance and contentment.

Yes, Lynn felt very comfortable there even under the circumstances. She instantly felt a sense of warmth and family and maybe a little deja-vu. Why, she had no idea, except CJ had been talking about his childhood and his time spent at Raven Hill with his playmate Billy Rob Bowers. Oh, how glad she was that CJ agreed to let them spend the night. He would never hear her complain about Raven Hill again.

"Lynn, Lynn, are you okay?"

Lynn was being called back to reality by the alarm in CJ's voice.

"Oh, Honey, I'm fine, I'm more than fine. I was just mentally drifting through thoughts about this place and how much I can now understand your love for it and all the memories. I can also understand why the Bowers clan was so protective of this land. I would give anything to be able to live off this land and enjoy the solitude it offers to its owner."

"Okay, that's enough dreaming. It's really not our cup of tea. We have the old homestead and that's close enough to Raven Hill for me, maybe even too close anymore."

"What do you mean by that remark, CJ?"

"Nothing, let's just warm up some chow and try real hard to relax."

CJ lit a small fire in the fireplace to warm up some soup and water for tea. Even though it was summer, it was summer in the mountains and the temperature is known to drop like a rock at nightfall and become chilly. CJ always thought it was cold on Bowers Mountain, at least it was now that he was grown and facing dilemmas he never could have imagined would be staring him in the face.

Since CJ had been to the cabin and spent time with Sheridan before he was hospitalized, he was pretty much aware where things were kept. He also knew that Lynn always liked to have tea with her meals and that would mean a trip out to the springhouse for milk. He never seemed to care for the taste of milk in tea. He was under the impression that it was an acquired taste from Europe.

He opened a couple of cans of soup and hung them on the fire hook in the fireplace. Lynn was in her own world, sitting on the old sofa and watching the fire. She had offered to help him, but he was glad to prepare the food. It gave him something to think about other than the events of the day. Lynn spoke, thanking CJ for letting them stay the night. She told him she was feeling much better, a little hungry and tired but not nauseous and achy. He was glad to hear that, maybe the stomach bug she was feeling was finally going to leave her system. He hoped he didn't catch it. It seemed like they were so close that they shared all things, good and bad.

"Lynn, I've got to go out to the springhouse to get some milk for tea. Keep your eye on the soup so it doesn't boil over, okay?"

"Sure, or I can go with you and we can move the soup over to the cool side of the fireplace. I bet the moon is gorgeous from here."

"Yeah, right", CJ said to himself, "and maybe those damn ravens will fly down and pluck out your eyes, too."

"Can we check out the moon together, CJ, on the walk to the springhouse?"

"No, not this time, babe. I want you to promise me you'll stay right where you are till I return with your milk, okay?"

CJ picked up a small glass that was in the drainer on the sink. Donnie and his pa had really been cleaning the old place up while they stayed with Sheridan. It was truly in pretty good shape. Most all the glass items in the cabin were shining from the glow of the fireplace and lanterns. It seemed much brighter, even though it was night.

Looking over to where Lynn was sitting, CJ realized that the moon was reflected in the large mirror that hung on the wall over in the corner of the room. That moon shone so brightly and the mirror was so clean that CJ could see the face of the moon. What has happened in one day that seems to have changed the whole feel of the mountain? Even the moon is able to shine through the trees and add comfort to an eerie place like Raven Hill. CJ kept his thoughts to himself.

"I'm going now. I hope to be right back with the milk, Lynn."

CJ took a deep breath and prayed for courage as he reached for the back door. He opened it just a crack; that would allow him the ability to see the springhouse as well as the cemetery and the ravens nesting in the old oak tree. To his surprise there were no ravens, only the bright glow of the moon shining over Bowers Mountain, as though peace itself had moved into this humble area and decided to take up residence.

CJ cautiously walked toward the springhouse to get the milk. It was so quiet he could hear the cheepers singing in the woods. He was sure he could even hear the water in the springhouse slowly running across the overspill on its way down the mountain. There was always a great supply of clear, fresh water on Bowers Mountain.

As kids he and Billy Rob always drank straight from the creek. Pa Bowers would say, "If you can see the frogs and waterbugs playing in the water, it's safe to drink. The water was vibrant with life and purity then and now. CJ opened the springhouse door and shined his flashlight inside. The frogs jumped into the water and he reembraced his clean water thoughts.

He looked at the perishable supplies that were lined up in a wooden box that was partially submerged in the water, removed the bottle of milk, and poured a small amount into the glass he had. He could see that Donnie had generously kept supplies on hand for Sheridan. There was butter, apple juice, milk, and even buttermilk, a drink that Sheridan so often would enjoy when CJ would visit them as a child. Sheridan would always offer the buttermilk to Billy Rob and CJ. The first time they tried it, thinking it must be good if Pa Bowers liked it so, they both gulped down a large mouth full of the chunky dairy brew, and they both spit it out and gagged over its distinctive taste and texture. After that Pa Bowers always offered them a swig. They would decline and he would laugh and slap his knee.

CJ backed out of the springhouse and slowly walked toward the cabin. From somewhere deep inside of him tears welled in his eyes and fell to his cheeks. He stopped and wept like a child. He could feel the loss of everyone he had ever loved, especially the Bowers family members. He was loved by all of them - the older boys, who were like brothers to him, Ma Bowers, who would set a place at the dinner table for him and clean off his scraped elbows and knees with gentleness and love, Billy Rob, who he loved dearly.

They were blood brothers and CJ was there to watch as they buried him in the family plot. He knew a little of his heart went with his mountain brother that day. Now only Pa Bowers was left and he was fighting a battle of life and death .CJ wanted so to be able to help him, but this battle was in God's hands. He did not want Pa Bowers to lose, but he knew Sheridan loved God above everything and everyone.

The truth was that CJ did not want to close the door on his childhood memories, and as long as Pa

Bowers still drew breath, Billy Rob, his brothers, and Ma Bowers still lived, loved and worshipped on Bowers Mountain and CJ would be able to always relive his childhood, because Pa was still there and alive. He continued to cry quietly for a second or two, then he heard Lynn calling to him. She was concerned, he had taken longer than she thought he needed to.

"CJ, are you alright? Is that you in the shadows?"

"Yes, I got the milk and I'll be right in. I was just admiring the moon light and got carried away in thought. I'm sorry, babe."

"It's ok, I can see how that would happen."

Lynn went back inside and CJ wiped his eyes and prayed for God's peace over Pa Bowers.

While CJ was out getting milk for the tea, Lynn had found some peanut butter and grape jelly and made some great sandwiches to go along with the hot soup. Tea was in the cups and CJ was carrying the milk into the cabin. The two of them sat down at the old handmade table and just stared at each other for a second. They were hungry and tired, but united in strength and love. They gave grace for the food they had and they prayed for Sheridan's healing and peace as he rested in the hospital.

After they had eaten, CJ opened up his wallet and took out the hospital card Dr. Miles had given him and his cell phone to call Central Memorial Hospital. He dialed the number and a woman's voice answered, announcing the hospital. CJ asked if he could please speak with someone in ICU in regard to Sheridan Bowers' condition. The receptionist transferred him to ICU and a nurse answered the call.

"Yes, Head nurse Robin Stewart, ICU, may I help you?"

CJ hesitated, then said, "Yes, please, my Father was airlifted there early today. His name is Bowers, Sheridan Bowers. Please, can you tell me if he is doing any better?"

"Well, there is no mention on his chart about a son, but Dr. Miles did mention at the change of shift meeting that a Claude John Rolley would probably be calling. You must be an adopted son."

"Yes, yes, that's right. Now, please, how is he doing?"

"Well, he is resting comfortably and still receiving IV fluids with antibiotics. The doctor ordered oxygen to help him breathe easier and that should make it easier on his heart, also. We are watching and measuring his vital signs and his input and output. I guess you could say he is holding his own for now. We will know better after 24 hours of care. Excuse me for one minute."

CJ could hear the nurse talking but he could not hear the conversation.

"Mr. Rolley, are you still there?"

"Yes," replied CJ.

"That was not about your father's condition. Please forgive me for making you hold. Call back tomorrow after 10 o'clock. That's when the doctors usually finish their rounds and you should be able to talk to Dr. Miles and he'll update you then."

"Thank you for your time and help, nurse. It will help my wife and I to rest easier. Tomorrow we will visit Pa."

"Bye, Mr. Rolley, and you're welcome."

As the nurse was hanging up the phone Sheridan was being moved across the hall, into another room where it was quieter and the private nurse wasn't so uncomfortable.

"Wow," said the aides as they passed the head nurse, "we have never seen such a gathering of crows on a window ledge. They seemed to be talking to each other as they flapped their wings. If that glass wasn't tempered they would probably be in the room raising cain and crapping all over. That's really weird."

"They are probably drawn to the electrical wires overhead coming into the hospital. I saw pictures of many birds out West sitting on just one section of wire, it's something to do with the electrical field some wires produce. Stop making a mountain out of a mole hill and go back to work, thank you. I'll close off that room and hope we won't need it tonight. We'll let the electricians figure it out tomorrow. It's not our problem."

Sheridan had no idea of what was happening, or that he had been moved from across the hall because of the birds gathering on the window ledge. He was peacefully sleeping while his body worked overtime to try and heal itself. Breathing was labored even with the oxygen flowing into his lungs. He had been in this condition for so long that his whole system was exhausted from fighting off the infection. It seemed like he was running out of energy or maybe just tired of living sick and alone. Whatever was going to happen was between him and his maker.

The doctors could do no more and the staff was at his side doing all they could to make him comfortable by administering prescribed medication. It was going to be a long wait and see.

CJ and Lynn moved to the sofa to finish their cups of tea and to talk. CJ explained to Lynn what the nurse had told him. They just looked at each other without speaking. Each sipped their tea and surveyed the room. The room was exactly how it was when he was a child. He remembered the sofas, tables, and even the chairs. His eyes went to the hearth by the fireplace where he had sat many times as a kid. He and the Bowers boys would whittle sticks and polish gun stocks. They would carve all sorts of everyday things from left over wood scraps, things like spoons, forks and ladles. Being carpenters, they never wasted wood.

Wood was considered a God-given gift, so waste not, want not. When they finished a large quantity of wooden what-nots, the boys would load them up in the truck for Pa to take to town and sell along with the furniture. That's how they would get some spending money. Boys needed things like knives, fishing hooks, and let's not forget shells, there was always hunting to be done.

CJ could mentally picture the whole family gathered around the big old kitchen table eating supper and then later talking about the events of the day. The best part of all is that he could see himself there, yeah, him and his buddy, Billy Rob. Pa Bowers used to tell his boys, "Someday this will all belong to you, my sons. After you boys this will be passed to your children." Pa never realized it would come to a point where he would out live his wife and sons.

"It's just not natural," CJ thought, "it's not natural, that the Bowers clan would work this mountain for generations and then go and give it to a Rolley."

CJ never realized how much this clan of mountain carpenters loved him, or how much he loved them. He broke from his train of thought and glanced over to his right side to speak to Lynn. While he had been deep in his own past, she had placed her tea cup on the end table and had fallen asleep. CJ stood up and placed her feet on the sofa and covered her with the afghan from the end of the sofa. She was soundly asleep and looked so relaxed. He watched her for a few seconds as she slept. Her chest would rise and fall so easily and rhythmically that he knew she was at peace and happy in her surroundings. Tomorrow morning they would call the hospital and find out how Sheridan was and how soon they could visit him. CJ knew he and Lynn would be up at the crack of dawn, which was probably a good thing. That would give them a chance to have a little breakfast, tidy up their mess, pick up their belongings, and head down the hill to reality.

CJ put a couple of small sticks of dry wood on the fire and settled down on the other sofa to rest. He had extinguished all the lanterns except the little one that was by Sheridan's rocker. The small table it sat on was the first one his son Max ever made. Max's passing was such a hurtful time, but it wasn't the last hurt to come for the old man, no, it was just the beginning in a long line of woes. Tough is the only way to label Pa Bowers and his bloodline. Five boys born into the family and all five gone.

One died in child birth, that was Thomas Alan. Then Jebidiah John, he crossed paths with a rattler and the snake won. Then was Max Jonas, he was struck down in a lightening storm. The flash was so great it singed his necklace and burned the tree image from the necklace into his skin. Then came Rufus Ray, he lost his life to the saw mill. Seems he lost his footing one day as he was working and fell forward. That old saw was sharp and fast, faster then he could move his arm. They stopped the bleeding but not the infection. He just never recovered from the shock to begin with. Next was Billy Rob, the youngest and last.

It was a hot, steamy summer day and Billy Rob had fed and watered the critters in the outbuilding as he had always done. Once he finished his chores he was allowed to go off into the woods to play and make discoveries. He wanted to learn how to work the saw but Pa said he was too young to swing and cut wood. The truth was, he was being sheltered from harm and death. It had visited four times before and it had left Ma and Pa Bowers leery. Time would pass some and Billy Rob would grow some and Ma and Pa would surely be able to accept the passing of the other boys and allow Billy his dream. Time did not pass much till the grim reaper was at the cabin door again.

Billy found a bee hive and, as boys will be, he pegged it with sticks and stones and the bees attacked. Pa found him late in to the evening swollen up three times his size and gone. Ma Bowers just could not take the loss. She gave up eating and drinking and she told Pa the night before she died, she was going to look for the boys and care for them. Pa understood she was broken. He buried her and went on living solo, waiting for his time to join them in paradise.

CJ could not help but wonder if this was Pa Bowers' time. He again glanced over to where Lynn was sleeping and could see she was fine. He looked up at the mantel with the rack of shot guns just above it and smiled a heart breaking smile. Without his realizing it, he fell off into a deep, well needed sleep, literally wrapped up in his memories by the blanket he used as a child on the sofa he always rested on with Billy Rob his blood brother.

Chapter Six

*T*he next day was beautiful and sunny and warm. It was pushing 10 o'clock when CJ was awakened by the bright ray of sunshine in his face. The same mirror that reflected the moon's glow the night before was now blinding him with the light of day. Lynn was stirring, but she was still asleep, and CJ did not believe it was very late. He stoked up the fireplace for morning coffee and tea at the same time the clock chimed 10 AM. He swung around to witness the time. How could they have possibly slept so long and so peacefully. At that moment CJ reached for the cell phone and the hospital card, he had to know how Pa was doing. Lynn was waking up and looking well refreshed.

"Wow, 10 o'clock, how long have you been up CJ?"

"I just got up, too. I can't believe it, either. Let me call the hospital and then I'll make you a cup of tea."

"You call and I'll make tea and coffee this time. I feel great and I want to."

CJ was into his phoning and said nothing in response. Lynn headed toward the sink and the hand pump.

"Hi, Central Memorial, may I please have the ICU desk? Hi, Nurse Martin, would it be possible to talk with Dr. Miles about Sheridan Bowers condition? Yes I'm his son, Claude John. Thank you, I'll wait."

As CJ was on the phone, Lynn was doing just fine making coffee and tea. She quietly opened the back door and was greeted by the sweet mountain air and the bright warm sun. Grabbing a clean cup she went to the springhouse for milk. CJ was so involved talking with the doctor he never realized she left. She was in love with this place, especially in the daylight.

Lynn opened the door and again the frogs jumped into the cool water. She was amazed at all the goodies the wooden box held. She took the milk, butter and juice out of the liquid fridge and started back to the cabin slowly, just looking around and deep breathing some of that mountain air into her lungs.

CJ was being told by Dr. Miles that Sheridan showed little improvement overnight. The doctor was not surprised by that, for the old man was a long time sick and it would take time to heal if he could. The doctor told CJ that it was foolish for him and Lynn to come to visit today. Sheridan was out of it and the trip would be in vain at this time.

"Do whatever else must be done. Think positive about his recovery and prepare for the time he may be able to return home. If he's fortunate for that to happen, CJ, he will not be able to be alone for quite some time, if ever. Maybe you and Lynn should think about how you two will handle this dilemma."

CJ thanked the doctor and agreed that they would not visit, but if there was a change in Sheridan's condition, the doctor would phone them immediately, be it good or bad. The doctor and CJ were in full agreement when CJ closed his cell phone.

He called out to Lynn, "Where are you?"

His pulse raced thinking she went outside and he hadn't made time to see if the ravens had returned to the oak tree. Why did he not look as soon as he awoke? He and Lynn reached the back door at the same time.

"Are you ok, Lynn?"

"Yes, of course I am. I went to get milk from the springhouse and found a small grocery store of goods there. Here, help me put these on the table."

As he lifted the milk and juice from her arms, Lynn asked how Mr. Bowers was doing.

"Well, Dr. Miles said that there was little change from yesterday, if any. He advised us not to make the trip in today because Sheridan was still unresponsive. He raised a good thought, too."

"What's that, CJ?" asked Lynn.

"What are we going to do if Sheridan pulls through this? He will want to come home and he can't be by himself at first and maybe never."

"Well, I'm sure we can cross that bridge when we have to. Together we can do just about anything Claude John Rolley Bowers."

Although the thoughts of Sheridan's coming home were overwhelming, the child in CJ could not and would not allow his mind to accept a negative outcome, meaning that he would pass on. Mr. Bowers was CJ's gateway to his childhood days and he loved his childhood, he loved Raven Hill and he especially loved the Bowers and the knowledge that he was one of them. It was as though they had adopted him and made his life full and wonderful. Yes, in his heart Sheridan Bowers was no plain mountain man, he was CJ's adopted father and he loved him in spite of the trials he was facing. He loved them all and he was proud to be one of them.

CJ had again drifted deep into his own world and thoughts. Lynn knew that blank stare on his face and she continued to busy herself with making breakfast. She was feeling pretty good and was glad that the bug she had caught had finally decided to leave her body. She had great plans for cleaning up the place and making it more comfortable. A little airing out would not hurt either and the day promised to be a beauty. Lynn scrambled a large pan of eggs, and that, along with coffee and juice, was looking like a regal spread and she was starved.

CJ was romanced back to reality by the smell of the eggs cooking and the fresh coffee. He moved up to the table to enjoy the bounty that Lynn had prepared. He could see the sun dancing through her long hair. He laughed to himself about how relaxed she must be here in Serpentine Gulch, even with all this drama going on. He knew that if they were back home, Lynn would have been to the beauty parlor a week ago. Her dark roots were starting to show, and her blonde hair was not so blonde anymore. In his eyes she was a keeper no matter what color her hair was, and her hair wasn't the only change he noticed in her. Her features had taken on a soft glow and her eyes glistened as she looked up at him while doling out a large portion of scrambled eggs on his plate. They both sat quietly and savored the food and each other's company. Occasionally one or the other would remark about the solitude and the beauty of Raven Hill. Lynn interjected that the beauty would be much more noticeable once she cleaned the windows.

"I thought that we would return to our own place today. I could leave you there and return daily to clean and fix up this place. I can't imagine you want to stay here and I don't know if it's a good idea anyhow."

"Why would I not want to stay and help you? And why is it not a good idea?" Lynn still had a sense that there was something more than CJ wanted to tell her about Raven Hill.

"Well," stammered CJ, "you're just starting to feel better, and this place really needs to be cleaned thoroughly. Besides that, there are wild animals up here to consider. I would not want you to get bitten or hurt, nor would Sheridan want that either."

What he really wanted to say was that this place had a bad omen hanging over it and if, no, he thought, when the ravens return he did not want her subjected to their attacks. Where they had gone worried him.

"CJ, don't be silly. I love it up here and I want to stay and help you. It would be foolish for you to drive up and down this mountain everyday. When we're apart all we do is think and worry about each other. I'm fine, see, I ate like a horse today and I'm ready to start cleaning, so finish up your eggs and get going outside to do your work so I can get started in here."

Lynn bent over and gave CJ a kiss and a smile .He was unable to not obey her demands. As always she was right, at least about the missing and worrying part. He was sure that they suffered separation anxiety when not together. Lynn had CJ fill the cauldron out in the fire pit with water for cleaning. He started a fire in the stone ring and then continued to clean the front porch. Good items not needed for everyday use were taken to one of the outbuildings. CJ returned each item to its rightful place as best as he could remember from when he was a kid.

He could feel himself growing younger with each trip to the outbuildings, and the good memories flowed through his mind, as if a dam broke and cascaded water over the land. He was happy to be there and happier to be helping Sheridan.

From the fire pit CJ could hear Lynn singing and he could see her flittering about as she cleaned the cabin. She had opened all the doors and windows to air out the place and she had made several trips to the cauldron for hot water. CJ had finished cleaning the porch and it looked very welcoming. He placed two rockers on the porch and a small table nestled between them. Lynn did not want him inside the cabin until she called him.

CJ wandered from shed to shed peering in and taking account of what was in each. At times he would restack some wood or move a piece of equipment to another space in the shed. The outbuildings were clean and quite tidy. The woodworking tools all had a place and they were in them. It looked as though

Sheridan had tried to keep the tools well oiled so they would not rust even though his illness had prevented him from returning to the sheds as often as he should have.

CJ looked around until he found some oil and some rags and he started to wipe down the tools. He wanted to show respect and love for his mountain father and brothers who made and loved their trade. He had opened the double doors on the tool shed and he sat with the sun beaming down on the trees and cabin. With the sun high in the sky the place looked so peaceful and serene. Even the cemetery had taken on a heavenly, peaceful stillness.

With the ravens gone, CJ realized he could hear the other birds singing in the trees. He could even see colorful little birds on the clothesline where Lynn had hung items to air out or dry in the sweet breeze. It was wonderful, he thought. He could see why the Bowers loved it here and he knew Pa Bowers would love to come back here to finish out his days on earth. If only there was a way to grant that wish. It all depended on Pa Bowers' will to live.

Chapter 7

*B*ack at the hospital, Pa Bowers was clinging to life, his body so depleted by the pneumonia, dehydration and age that it was not looking too good for him. His body was fighting to obey his mind. Sheridan Bowers never gave up easily, and he would not make any exceptions this time, either. As he lay motionless in the hospital bed, the electric company and the hospital grounds men were fighting a losing battle to remove the ravens from the window sills. It had started with one window sill at the same time Sheridan was admitted and it grew to the point that the ravens were taking up residence on that entire side of the hospital.

The electric company had done all they could do. They relocated lines and junctions into the building and nothing seemed to discourage the birds from the sills. It was amazing to the linemen that they could work around the ravens and in the midst of them with no combat between man and fowl, but they would not leave the area. Poison was placed on the sills and they would kick it off or push it off with their wings. Loud speakers were placed at different intervals on the building playing owl sounds. With owls being their predator you would think it would work. The ravens appeared to ignore all things done to frighten them away. It was as though they were soldiers on an assignment, but, to do what, was the question on the minds of all who wanted them gone.

It had become such a battle between the hospital and the birds that it made the local papers. Many would come to see these birds sitting on the window sills. They seemed to be trying to look into the hospital rooms. For what reason, no one knew. It was foolish to think they were stalking patients. The nursing staff had ordered the blinds be closed, it was making the patients uneasy. Since admittance, Sheridan was relocated to the other side of the hospital. As the birds originally gathered on the windowsill of his room, the staff moved him and closed off the room, thinking it would be the only area affected because several electrical junctions entered the wall at that room. In time it has proven not to be an issue of electrical current. It just was and only the ravens knew why.

Sheridan was oblivious to the ravens on the window sills or that he was moved because they were outside of his hospital window when he was first admitted. He was in a life and death struggle, and right now he was losing. Alarms and monitors were screaming for medical attention in his room. He was entering another crisis; he was having a stroke. Dr. Miles was being paged over the hospital loud speaker, "Dr. Miles, report to Room 312 stat, code blue. Medical alert, Dr. Miles report to Room 312 stat, code blue." All personnel was on the run to room 312, including Dr. Miles. Immediately he orchestrated the life saving symphony that would again stabilize Sheridan's health. Blood was drawn, x-rays taken, lungs checked and rechecked, body responses tested. He was once again holding his own, but no one, not even Dr. Miles, would know what had happened or what effect it would have on the old man's body and recovery until the test results came back. The doctor could see no reason to alert CJ and Lynn at this time. Sheridan was stable and the verdict was out on the test until morning.

Hours ago CJ and Lynn had lunch out under a large oak tree, and they now lay resting in the shade with full stomachs and peace embracing them as they enjoyed the quietness and the warm, fragrant air of the mountain. They had accomplished an amazing amount of work. The sheds were in order and the tools had all received a fresh coating of oil. Each item was in its original place and there seemed to be a spirit of contentment that occupied the outbuildings.

The cabin was as clean and fresh as Mrs. Bowers would have kept it. Lynn had worked the better part of the day scrubbing and washing. The entire space was so clean you could smell the pine cleaner that was used to remove years of dust and grime. Every window and mirror and piece of glassware shone and sparkled with love. It was an amazing transformation, from a neglected, forgotten homestead, to a newly resurrected place of love, respect and family values. Every part of the cabin was aglow, except for one very small room that held important documents and papers, plus personal items, such as family albums and bibles with important dates and events listed on the inside of the covers. There was also some of Ma Bowers jewelry and trinkets, baby blankets and clothes from the past, and Ma Bowers' wedding dress packed away with Pa Bowers' wedding attire.

Lynn just did not think it was right for her to enter this private domain. Everything in there was old, but pristinely packed and placed to last forever. This room really was Raven Hill and it was sacred. The only people who should enter in, Lynn thought, were Sheridan, and in time, CJ. She was so tempted to snoop as she was cleaning and shining the cabin, but for some reason a side of her would not allow her to do more then crack the door and look.

CJ and Lynn slept soundly in the warm late afternoon sun. They stirred only when the sun started to slide down the mountainside to take rest so the moon could cast its light on the stars and cause them to twinkle. The night was surely upon them; the day had been perfect and well appreciated by them. They had completed so much cleaning and organizing that the old homestead again stood proudly in the midst of the trees.

Just as Sheridan was being stabilized and on his way back to health, Raven Hill was also under going changes. Old Man Bowers would surely see Raven Hill again and life would return to its humble beginnings. At least that was the hope and dream of CJ, Lynn, and Dr. Miles.

CJ and Lynn truly needed the nap on the lawn. CJ looked around at the homestead and felt a sense of great pride and respect. He knew that when Sheridan returned it would do his heart good to see the old place again rising out of its shambles much like the mythical Phoenix. The two of them gathered up their uneaten cheese, fruit and bread they had shared for lunch, and pushed themselves to fold the blanket and head for the cabin before night was totally upon them.

Inside CJ lit several glass lanterns and proceeded to close windows and doors keeping the cool night air and unwelcome insects out. The cabin was beautifully fresh and the lantern light made everything sparkle and glow. The couple sat on the sofa reliving the events of the day. Lynn seemed far away as CJ spoke to her about the condition he found the sheds in. He talked about returning things to their rightful places as he remembered from his childhood. He smiled to himself as he spoke out loud. When there was no response or interest shown by Lynn, CJ turned to look at her. That's when he realized she was miles away mentally.

"Lynn," he said, as he tapped her on the arm, "are you ok?"

"Yes, yes, I'm fine, just thinking about the future."

"What future?" asked CJ.

"Pa Bowers' future. Listen to me, CJ, and be open minded and patient as I speak to you."

"OK, lady;" was the reply, but there was hesitancy in his voice.

"When Sheridan is well enough to be released from the hospital, he will never want to live anywhere but here. If you think about it there is nowhere around here that would take him in. There are no nursing homes in this area, families take care of their own. Right?"

"Yeah, that's true. No one can argue with that."

"We are his only family, CJ. Let's rent out our home and move here and tend to Sheridan's needs. The house would continue to be ours and the rent would carry it. We have some money in savings and once you put the mill in operation again and start making furniture with the Raven Hill logo on it, we will be quite comfortable, and Sheridan will be home and happy."

"Do you realize what you are saying, Lynn? It's a hard life up here, especially in the winter months. We may not be able to go to town for several weeks if the snow fall is great. What if Sheridan needed medical care, like before?"

"We would again call for medical air lift. They know where they're going now."

As much as CJ loved the idea, he knew how rough it was to live in the mountains, especially when winter came. His mind was racing with pros and cons of such an endeavor. It seemed to be the perfect answer, but what would Sheridan think about such an invasion of his private space, and yet what would he do and where would he go if this was not workable.

Lynn handed CJ a glass of cool tea that had brewed in the cold beverage crock that was probably 100 yrs old or older. He sipped it and thought, "what if", and "how could they", and money, and jobs and possibilities and Sheridan's health etc, etc, etc. Lynn just continued to tidy up.

There were a few pieces of cheese and some grapes left from lunch, plus a small tearing of bread. Normally she would have saved it for tomorrow, but she was hearing and feeling a rumbling stomach so she picked and munched until all the lunch leftovers were nicely consumed and her stomach was satisfied and content.

CJ remarked that he was not sure about this undertaking. There was a lot to consider, so it was best to sleep and pray on it as they waited for Sheridan to make the next move. That night they decided to sleep in the main bedroom. Lynn had clean sheets on the bed and the room and its fragrance was inviting. With the window slightly ajar to catch the cool breeze from the mountain side, the couple slept like babies, in the arms of the Lord. Sheridan, too, slept well as his body recouped from the stroke he suffered earlier that day.

Morning brought bright sunshine and the promise of another beautiful summer day. Lynn and CJ were up and enjoying their first hot cup of tea and coffee. CJ had restarted the wood stove in the kitchen and the bacon was frying, sending a mouthwatering aroma throughout the cabin. It was so surreal to CJ and he loved it so. Lynn had slipped out to the springhouse to get some orange juice and butter from the liquid fridge. She was side tracked by a wave of nausea that took her to the backside of a large oak tree. She did not want to worry CJ and she did not want to do anything that would tarnish the possibility of moving to Raven Hill. She loved the natural living and she knew she had overdone the day before. After all, that cold or flu she had caught really slowed her down and the stress of the vacation didn't help either. As she calmed herself she realized it was also time for her monthly friend, and that always made her nauseous and crampy. Well, I've got the nausea, so I'm sure the cramps will start soon.

As she continued walking to the springhouse to retrieve the juice and butter, she thought of how glad she was that the main cleaning was done. The smell of bacon was in the air, and it only added to her queasiness. She was able to handle it and with juice and butter in hand she started back toward the cabin.

Today they would probably go to town to visit Sheridan and talk to Dr. Miles. She would have to get more supplies and she'd better pick up more personal hygiene needs, because this was going to be her womanly week. As Lynn entered the kitchen door, CJ was cracking the eggs into the pan.

"How many do you want Lynn, 2 or 3?"

"Oh, I'll have none, I mean one. One is more than enough. I ate too much yesterday and my clothes won't fit if I don't slow down."

"Are you sure, Babe? One will hold you?"

"I'm more than sure."

In her mind she wasn't even able to eat it so this was going to be a real challenge. The eggs were frying and Lynn was sipping her tea to quiet her stomach. CJ placed two plates on the table, one with one egg and 3 slices of bacon was put in front of Lynn, and 3 eggs and a stack of bacon was on the plate in front of CJ. Lynn turned a little green at the sight of breakfast, but CJ sat down and asked Lynn, "Do you really want to live here and care for Sheridan with me? The winters can be brutally cold and long. Many people, if they are not accustomed to it, suffer from cabin fever. You kinda go stir crazy."

"Do you really think we could cover all the expenses that will occur?"

"Lynn, I'm so torn by this whole situation. I want to do what is right for all, but you are my first priority. I love you more than life, and I don't want to drag you into something we will regret. I don't want to put a strain on our relationship."

"CJ, it's what I want, too. We can do this, we can do anything we put our minds on to do. Maybe it's not what other young couples would like or want. To us it's answered prayer. You always loved working with wood, and you're good at it even though you don't think so. Maybe you're not up to a Bowers logo yet, but in time, and when that time comes, think about adding a raven that's wearing a capital R to the logo tree branch, showing a new member of the family has restarted the furniture production." "We may be counting our chickens before they hatch, Lynn."

"Why would you say that? Excuse me but if Sheridan lives or, or, you know, passes on, Raven Hill will still be yours. That's what you told me he said."

CJ could not remember telling her that, but it would not be unusual that he did, he told her everything. Just at that moment his cell phone rang. CJ rustled it out of his pants pocket, opened it, and put it to his ear.

"Hello, hello."

"Hello, CJ", said Dr. Miles.

"Is Sheridan ok?" asked CJ.

"Well, he had a rough time yesterday."

"Why didn't you call me?" CJ asked.

"There was nothing for you do. We were able to stabilize him and run some tests. I pretty much diagnosed his problem, but without some tests to confirm my thoughts, I could not say for sure. Now the tests results are back and we know Mr. Bowers suffered a stroke, and it was quite a devastating one. He has very little use on his dominant side, which means his right side, and I'm sorry to say he is unable to speak. The tests and the MRI show clearly that a large part of his brain was involved.

"Now this does not mean he will never walk or talk again, but it does mean he will need a great deal of help and loving patience. That's assuming he comes though this. So far he is definitely holding his own, and that's a lot. CJ, I'm not a betting man, but if Bowers shows any improvement in the next 24 hours I think he'll make it. Have you and Lynn done any thinking on what you're going to do in the event he survives?"

"We are going to stay here and care for him and we will love him back to health."

"Well, I don't think you should be looking for any miracles of complete healing at his age, but for him to return to reality and semi-clear thinking would be wonderful. He is one tough mountain man."

"Lynn and I will be in today to see him doctor."

Well, I've got him totally sedated and resting, so he will not know you've been here. I don't think at this time he would recognize you anyhow. He'll be fuzzy thinking for a few days at least. Continue to work on your moving plans. Before you know it, fall will be here and Mr. Bowers will hopefully be on his way home."

"Dr. Miles, we'll take your suggestion and work on getting ready for Sheridan's homecoming."

"Good," he replied, "then I'll call as soon as I see a change in Mr. Bowers' condition."

All the while the doctor was talking, CJ could hear people in the background commenting on the birds doing something, or maybe it was a television program he was overhearing, but he had to ask.

"Wait, doctor, wait. I'm hearing a lot of confusing talk about birds as we speak. What is that, a documentary someone is watching?"

"I wish it was. For some inexplicable reason the south side of the hospital is home to hundreds of black birds. They have taken up living here for days. They came about the same time your friend did and they refuse to leave no matter what is done to discourage it. They just try to peer into the hospital windows. They don't hurt anyone coming or going, but they are a health issue, if you get my drift."

"Yeah, I do," said CJ.

"I'll be in touch. Bye for now."

"Yeah, bye for now, Dr. Miles."

"Well, how is Sheridan?" asked Lynn.

CJ was holding back a gnawing fear that he did not want to entertain. He knew the birds were ravens and they were keeping a vigilant watch out for Sheridan. They must sense he was still alive, because they were still there.

"Oh, Sheridan, he suffered a bad stroke yesterday and it seems to have left him paralyzed on his right side and unable to speak. Dr. Miles says he's stabilized now and holding his own. The doctor seems to think that he has a chance of surviving. He's really strong willed."

With tears in his eyes and a foreboding feeling in his soul, CJ walked outside to calm himself and breathe the fresh air. He thought it might clear his thoughts and allow him to grasp what was happening and why. He would not tell Lynn about the birds, not until he had to and he hoped that would never happen.

Lynn finished tidying up the cabin and then she walked outside to enjoy the day and be with CJ. There was a noticeable change in the air; fall was right around the corner and getting ready to make its debut. Lynn snuggled up to CJ's back as he glanced over the outbuildings and cemetery.

"It's starting to cool down up here on the mountain," said Lynn.

"The sun will be high in the sky soon and things will warm up again."

"Are we going into town today?" she asked.

"We can. Is there something we need or we're out of?"

"Well, we could certainly use some more supplies and it's that time of the month for me. Need I say more?"

"No, I understand you. You know, if we're going to stay here, we'll have to make a few large investments."

"Like what?" Lynn asked.

"A gas powered generator to run a refrigerator and charge our cell phones. We also need a chain saw to cut wood for the stove and fireplace. We'll have to start hauling gas up the mountain now to hold us through winter. That means we need some storage tanks and we need to talk to Donnie and his Dad for help and also to update them on Sheridan's condition. Get what you need and close the door. I'll get the SUV and we can start heading to town."

Lynn went back into the cabin where she checked the kitchen stove and grabbed her shopping list. She picked up her purse and fumbled inside of it until she found a peppermint candy which she popped into her mouth, hoping it would calm her stomach. One last look around and out the door she went and up the small incline to the SUV and CJ.

All that was on CJ's mind was the birds and Sheridan. Their needs for the winter and renting out the house back home seemed trivial in comparison. As far as Lynn was concerned, CJ saw a happy woman who could not wait until they were moved in and settled. Only thing was she did not know about the birds and the history of Raven Hill.

Maybe CJ was making a mountain out of a mole hill, maybe it was all the responsibility that was thrust upon him that made him jump to conclusions. Then again, maybe he was not taking this as seriously as he should. Pa Bowers was dead serious about all matters regarding Raven Hill and his ancestry.

The ride back down the mountain was awesome and bumpy, but Lynn was doing okay. The butterflies in her stomach seemed to have left her. As they rode they made plans to stop at Donnie's first. CJ hoped he and his pa would take him to get the mechanical things he and Lynn would need to make it more comfortable up on Raven Hill. If they were open to helping CJ, it would mean using the pick-up truck to haul the items up the mountain trail. CJ had full intentions of paying them for their time and effort. Lynn would be free to grocery shop with the SUV, then later they would all meet for a good hot meal and some much needed down time.

They also discussed calling CJ's Mom and Dad, hoping they would be able to help with the renting out of their home. They would need to call their bank in hopes of refinancing before they actually rented the house. The bank had made offers in the past for lower rates or an equity loan and CJ and Lynn wanted to take advantage of it before they left their jobs.

She told CJ she would take care of work. They still had several weeks before they would have to come up with a reason to extend their time off. Hopefully the new loan would have gone through by then and renters would be lined up. The house would be rented fully furnished. CJ was sure his folks could box up their personal items and place them in the garage under lock and key until things could be thought out more clearly. It was workable in both their minds.

Lynn took the checkbook and CJ took the credit card. They had reached the landing at the bottom of the mountain; next stop was Donnie's place. Lynn was starving so she popped another peppermint into her mouth until she could steal away from the guys and have a burger meal on the way to the grocery.

It seemed too easy. As far as Lynn was concerned their dream was going along without a hitch. It would be perfect for her, CJ, and, of course, Sheridan

Bowers. From CJ's point of view it was going too well, things were falling into place too easily He did not want to be negative, but he knew it had to be a case of smoke and mirrors.

Chapter 8

*F*rom the base of the mountain to Donnie's house was not far. As expected, Donnie's truck was in his driveway. It would be unusual to find him and his pa not home. Their lives were very private and regimented. They spent most of their time in the early morning fishing, but as soon as the sun was locked into the sky they were home cleaning their fish and tying new lures for the next time.

In the fall and winter it was hunting. They were real sports minded men, and with no mates or children around to care for, their life was their own. Donnie and his pa were the best of friends. CJ worried to think of either of them passing and leaving the other on his own and lost.

As he swung the SUV into the driveway, out ran Pa and Donnie's two large, blue tick hounds. They must have been around back. Donnie followed the dogs around the side of the house and gave a wave of invitation to follow him. His hands were bloody and he had his fishing knife in his left hand. Just as always, he was cleaning fish for their meal .The dogs were used to Lynn and CJ because they lived just below in the Rolley cabin. Lynn would give the hounds table scraps and dog bones which she kept by the back door. She liked having them visit her although they were daunting to look at.

"Come on Lynn, let's go talk to Donnie and his pa."

"Oh, CJ, not if he's cleaning fish, that's too gross for me, please. I'll wait here until you see if they can help you get the things we need. Let me know if they can, then I can go shopping."

"OK, Lynn," and with that CJ disappeared around the side of the house.

Between being hungry and the thoughts of Donnie cleaning fish, Lynn's stomach did a roll over. Lynn saw one of the dogs coming toward the SUV and she put her hand out to rub its head. The hound approached the SUV and welcomed his ears being rubbed and he seemed to understand the words of friendship that Lynn was murmuring as she petted and stroked his head. About that time CJ came out the front door and headed toward the passenger side of the SUV.

"Donnie's pa and Donnie are more than happy to help us out. He's got a used oil tank behind his cabin that's cleaned out we can have for storage of gas. That will save us some there. They also know think they know where we can get a refrigerator and chain saw fairly cheap and in good shape from some guys they know. Donnie's pa knows good from bad. I'm worried about buying used goods, but I really don't think anyone in their right mind would try and pull a fast one on Donnie Joe or his pa.

"Why don't you go shopping, but get only non-perishable items today. I think maybe it would be best for us to stay here at our cabin tonight, then head back up the mountain tomorrow. Donnie thinks by then we will have the refrigerator, chain saw and generator, plus some gas to take back up to Raven Hill. If we get lucky, then early in the morning you can pick up perishables and have a place to keep them when we return to Raven Hill."

"Sounds good to me, CJ," was Lynn's response.

"Lets all meet back at our cabin here in town, and then we can figure out what to do for supper. Be careful, Honey, and as I score on items I'll phone you, and if I hear anything more about Sheridan I'll also call."

"OK, CJ, bye, and say 'hi' to the guys for me."

CJ called to the dogs and they followed him to the house as Lynn backed the vehicle out of the drive and headed to the next town over for a full size grocery store. She knew this was going to be a time consuming trip. There was a lot she wanted to stock up on. They had been eating pretty basically up on Raven Hill since this all started. There was no reason why a full, hearty meal could not be prepared. It was obvious that Mrs. Bowers made full-course meals, after all she had to cook large with all those men working hard, making furniture from scratch. Their appetites must have been out of sight.

Driving to the next town, Lynn pondered about Ma Bowers, and how hard it must have been for her up there. Lynn had seen where a vegetable garden had been. It would not have been a small job to keep it weeded and cultivated. There were also animals to care for, washing, cleaning, sewing, schooling and birthing. Lynn thought Ma Bowers must have been some woman. Yet, on the other hand, it was the life style of the times. There were no modern electrical gadgets to rely on. There was only you and your ability to be productive and inventive. Of course, once the kids were old enough they had chores to do, which helped some, but that was once they were old enough.

Lynn spotted a fast food place where she and CJ had stopped once before, and this was where she was going to stop now. She pulled up to the drive-thru menu and decided she would have a large burger, fries, and chocolate shake. As she ordered the meal, she could feel herself salivating over the thoughts of the feast to come. Lynn knew she was out of character, but she was starved. When she finished the ordering, a voice informed her that it would cost her $5.75 and please pull around to the second window for her order. Gladly she wheeled the SUV to the second window, where she paid her bill and then headed for a parking place, so she could dine. Lynn was careful not to inhale her meal, no matter how hungry she was.

Though she did not rush, she did not waste one bite or one fry. The slurping sound she was hearing indicated that no shake went to waste either. Lynn was full, happy, energized, and ready to take on the grocery shopping. With the trash from her meal placed in the outside waste can, she was on her way. The grocery store was about a block away. Once inside the parking area, she saw it was a good time for this undertaking. There were not that many cars in the lot so she was able to get up front for easy loading.

While Lynn was in the store doing her best to fill the pantry at Raven Hill, CJ and the guys were well on their way to do good also. The pick-up truck already had a fine looking refrigerator strapped in the bed. It was not the newest model, but it was good sized and well cleaned. The rubber gaskets on the doors were soft and pliable. Its freezer froze water and it was a steal. Next stop was to look at the chain saw. CJ was feeling good and he was thankful to have such good friends. After several hours of searching and trying equipment with Donnie and his Pa, the last thing they needed to purchase was a generator. Donnie drove to a farmer's outlet store. The sign about the door said "If we don't have it, we'll show you how to live without it." CJ chuckled to himself as they entered the door. Walking to the back of the store, there they were.

"Bingo," said Donnie.

The next thing was CJ handing over his credit card and Donnie and his pa loading the generator into the truck next to the refrigerator and the chain saw. The ride back to their side of life and their town was light and happy. The guys had made some wonderful deals and they were more than contented with their finds. CJ filled their gas tank at a small station on the way back, and they also partook of fast food delights. It was a long day and by the time they decided on where supper would be, they would be able to eat again without question.

Lynn was also doing well. She was able to hit a lot of sales. She also found that the store carried a large selection of canned meats, and full meals with meat in them. CJ was a good hunter so she was sure at some point they would have venison. If the guys did well she would be picking up fresh meats tomorrow.

She would first have to see how large the freezer compartment was before she bought any.

Lynn and Donnie pulled into the driveway just minutes apart. They all exited their vehicles and met at the back of the pick-up. Lynn was thrilled to see the goodies they had acquired and as they spoke about the cost of each item she was even more elated. Donnie and his Dad drove the pick-up over to their cabin where the dogs could keep an eye on it. Lynn and CJ needed to remove some of the groceries from the SUV so there was room for the four of them to go a restaurant and indulge in a nice, relaxing sit down meal.

With enough room for all in the SUV off they went to eat and enjoy each other's company. The time they spent together was great and the meals were tasty and filling. The ride back to the cabins at Serpentine Gulch was heavy and long. The subject was Sheridan Bowers and his health and life. He was loved and admired by all three men.

Lynn was not as moved emotionally by the talk as she did not have the same connections with Sheridan and Raven Hill as the three others did. Though she was grateful he loved CJ the way he did, and thrilled to be married to the future owner of Raven Hill, Lynn truly hoped that Sheridan would get better and be able to return to his beloved home. She was just concerned about the care he would need and the span of time he would need it for. She knew in her heart her thoughts were cold. Yet she and CJ had their lives ahead of them and they would not be free to establish and live on Raven Hill the way they would like with Sheridan present.

Once they arrived home they agreed to meet the next morning at 8 AM. The men would start back up the mountain with the mechanical and dry goods and Lynn would go to town again and select the perishables, then she would join them on Raven Hill. They all turned in early; tomorrow would be another full day and they never knew what was around the next turn or the next phone call. Lynn fell asleep almost as soon as her head hit the pillow.

Earlier that day, CJ had informed his friends about the birds and the hospital. Now that conversation would not let him sleep. He remembered how neither of them wanted to speak about Sheridan or the birds, but the ravens were not on Raven Hill and neither was Sheridan Bowers. The whole conversation proved to be unnerving to the three of them to the point that it was dropped and not given any more discussion. For the next hour CJ tossed and turned until exhaustion made his mind cease to ponder the question, "Why?"

They both slept soundly and peacefully. Having their bodies spooned together was probably one good reason for the restful rejuvenation, but surely they were tired emotionally and physically. Morning came and it was much welcome. The night's rest had been good and the four of them were ready to go. Fresh coffee and pastry buns were on the table.

Donnie and his pa were already enjoying their second cup of coffee when Lynn entered the kitchen. CJ had heard her moving about the bedroom so he prepared her a cup of tea. She was glad to be alive today, she felt wonderful and full of energy. She greeted everyone with a smile and a happy good morning and thanks to their neighbors for their time and help. Lynn had made up her mind to invite them up to Raven Hill for a nice supper. Maybe by that time Sheridan would be home and she thought he might like that also. It was obvious that the father and son had done a lot to keep Sheridan going until he had to be hospitalized.

CJ was returning his wallet and keys to the pockets of his jeans. He also picked up his cell phone and opened it to check for any calls he may have missed. The music played as he flicked the lid open, but thankfully there where no missed calls. Well, no news was good news, at least that was everyone's belief.

CJ had placed a couple of coolers in the back of the SUV and made Lynn fully aware of them. He reminded her to put some ice each of them. Between the ice and the coldness of the meat, there would be no problem with spoilage between town and Raven Hill. Sounded good to her, so she answered in the affirmative. All would be fine as long as the guys could get the refrigerator working, which meant the generator would have to work also. Well, if not she had heavy duty plastic bags and there was a great springhouse on Raven Hill. Ok, that would work no matter.

"Well, Babe, the guys and I are on our way up the mountain, we just want to stop for some gas for the generator and then it's full speed ahead. Is there anything else we can do for you before we leave?"

"No, I'm good. I'm going to take my time. I want to tidy up here and be sure everything is clean and neat, then I'll go to the store and buy some meats, milk and butter. You're going to have to think about being a true mountain man yourself, in time."

"What are you saying?"

"I'm saying, you'll have to get back to hunting, fishing, and trapping to provide meat for the table."

"Lynn, that's not a chore at this point in time, it's something I'm looking forward to."

"Good deal, my mountain man. Do be careful. I love you and I need you."

"You too, Baby, take your time. If there's a problem, please call me."

"Ok, go, the guys are waiting for you. That refrigerator must be cooled down when I get there."

"No problem," laughed CJ as he left the Rolley Homestead.

Lynn continued to tidy up and do the chores at hand. She was glad that CJ had dug out the coolers from the back room and placed them in the SUV. She finished all she had to do before she felt she could move on to the grocery store. The last thing she did was to empty the ice cube trays into the two coolers.

She figured that would give the coolers a chance to cool down before she placed the cold items into them along with more ice.

It was going to be a time consuming trip back up the mountain, and she would be traveling a little slower now with all the goods in the SUV. That cattle trail called a road really had dips and grooves in it. She did not want any broken bottles or jars, not in her vehicle.

Lynn took her time and shopped frugally, watching weight and price per pound on each meat item she purchased. Next was the fresh fruits; she wanted apples and oranges, maybe a melon, items that would have the longest shelf life, after all she had already bought a variety of canned fruit and vegetables. Last, but not least, she came to the veggie aisle. She could not wait until she could get her hands on some fresh broccoli and tomatoes, and, yes, green beans. Why she craved them so she didn't know, but, oh well, she did, so in her cart they went. She picked up butter on sale and a couple of gallons of fresh milk. Powdered milk was already packed in the SUV.

She thought for awhile and mentally rechecked her shopping list, but nothing more came to her mind, so with that she rolled the cart up to the checkout aisle where she retrieved two bags of ice. After waiting for her turn to bag up and pay out, she rolled the goodies to the SUV, where she loaded the coolers with the perishable meats first, then butter, milk, then what produce would fit. Room was limited in the coolers so what did not fit was fruit, some veggies, and eggs. Lynn loaded these items into double paper bags with plastic bags of ice packed with them so they would stay cool. It was good and it would work just fine.

As she climbed into her smorgasbord on wheels, she was really glad that CJ was able to get the items he went for cheaply, because this food trip topped off at four bills. Between yesterday and today, they had spent over a thousand bucks, and yet she thought it was still a good price for all they purchased.

Lynn started up the SUV and headed to the gas station for a fill-up before heading back to Raven Hill. As the attendant filled her vehicle, Lynn's thoughts were on CJ, Donnie, and Donnie's pa. They should be there by now. She hoped all would go well with the placing of the refrigerator and generator. Not to worry, there was nothing the three guys could not handle.

With the SUV topped off she was on her way. Lynn was really happy with the thought of living on Raven Hill. She would smile and laugh to herself about the prospects of having a large garden and some chickens and maybe a cow in time. And maybe, just maybe, a couple of horses down the road in time. Peace and quiet and no one in your face. No traffic and city noise, only birds and critters of the woods and wind humming through the trees. It was just too good. Of course there would be Sheridan to care for. Well, really, how long could that last under the circumstances? She would have to endure, and really, if it weren't for him, she would not be living at Raven Hill at all. "Oh well" was her thought. Just one more right turn and it's all up hill after that, and here we go. Next stop - home and CJ.

Chapter 9

*T*he ride up the mountain was slower then normal, but it would never be a fast trip. As Lynn rode she again mulled over all she bought and then realized the one thing she was going to need never made it to the cart. She forgot the pads for her monthly friend; yeah, she had a couple left from last month, but not enough. Well, she was sure they would be visiting Sheridan before too long.

The men had finished placing the generator and the refrigerator well before Lynn got back. The fridge was even cooled down and ready to accept its load of perishables. The generator was located a ways from the cabin so the noise would not be too disturbing as it ran making electricity. The guys also built a make shift barrier around and over it protecting it from the elements and adding to the quietness of its running. The one tank that Donnie was able to get in the truck was set upright and was the home for several gallons of gas which they brought along. The next time that Donnie and his dad came up they would bring the other tank and more gas. This was going to be a ritual between CJ and Donnie until both tanks were full for the winter months. That would be priority, gas and some kerosene for lamps; the kerosene only if for some reason the generator quit.

Lynn had packed a few electric lamps in the SUV for Raven Hill. It would be safer and cleaner, especially with Sheridan moving about. Just as Lynn crowned the top of the hill, CJ was receiving a call from Dr. Miles.

"Hi, CJ? Is that you?"

"Yes, Dr. Miles, go ahead, it's me."

"Well, I've got some good news. Mr. Bowers was removed from his sedative medicine last night and when he awoke this morning, he motioned he was hungry. We doctors here are astounded by his recovery. His lungs are much clearer and his vital signs are good, considering all things. He is unable to form words but he is trying hard and he can make sounds. His right side is without strength or movement but he's on the mend, I'd say."

"That's great doctor. When can we see him?"

"Well, your visiting time will be limited at this point, but how about tomorrow afternoon?"

"Great, we'll be there. Send him my concern and my, my..,"

"I will, CJ. See you tomorrow after your visit."

"Thanks again, Dr. Miles. I can't wait to tell his friends. Bye for now."

Lynn pulled the SUV down to the cabin and got out and headed toward the back. CJ and the men sauntered toward the cabin to help carry in the bounty that was in the vehicle.

"Hey, now that were all together, I want to tell you about the phone call I just received from Sheridan's doctor. It seems like the old boy woke up this morning looking for some breakfast. He was unable to speak words, but he could make noise and even with his right side affected by the stroke he made his wants known. I'm sure Dr. Miles explained to him the best he could what had happened to him. The doctor also said his lungs were sounding good and his vitals were good for what all he has been through. Lynn and I can visit him for a short time tomorrow, then you guys could go visit him the next day or whenever it would be convenient for you. I know he would really like to see both of you."

The men all cheered for the great recovery Sheridan was showing. Lynn just grabbed a couple of light bags and started toward the cabin. Once in, she cleared off the table and small counter top waiting for more bags to arrive via CJ, Donnie, and his pa. Lynn made lemonade as the men ushered the groceries in. The coolers were last to pass through the cabin door. Lynn used some of the ice from the produce bags to cool down the lemonade. She placed a large pitcher on a small table in the sitting room area and placed three large glasses by it so the guys could drink. Meanwhile she put away the cold items, and the refrigerator was cooling down nice. The freezer was at freezing and she smiled at the guys as they watched her pack food in.

The cabin was quite roomy. It had three bedrooms, one larger then the other two, plus, it had a floor to ceiling canned goods closet which was pretty deep and would hold a lot. In addition, there the smaller room where Sheridan's family treasures were stored. That room held an arsenal of gaming gear and shells.

Once Lynn finished putting away most of the bags of food, she stopped, washed her hands, and proceeded to set the table with fried chicken, potato and macaroni salads, pickles, chips, and eight tasty looking apple turnovers. She also mixed up a pitcher of iced tea.

"Come on guys, you deserve to eat. I hope it's OK. Please eat all you want."

The men moved from the sitting area to the table, each thanking her for the effort she went through to feed them. Lynn was then able to sit down and eat with them. Donnie's pa waited until all were seated and then he began to give thanks for the meal, the events of the day, and most of all for Sheridan and his healing. They all filled their stomachs, not leaving much to put away.

Lynn was glad they enjoyed it and looking at the little left, they did. CJ gave her a peck on the cheek and said he and the boys would be out by the sheds. He would gladly help her clean up later.

"No, go and relax with Donnie and his pa."

She was thrilled at the way they set up her kitchen and the electric lights were plugged in and ready to go. She cleaned up the dinner mess, poured herself a glass of iced tea, and started toward the front porch to rock and rest. She could see the guys working with the chain saw. One was cutting some wood and the other two had just finished stacking the wood left in the wood shed by Sheridan. There was a lot that was seasoned and ready to burn. Surely CJ would be adding to that pile before any of it would be needed in the fireplace.

The day was winding down and the chain saw stopped its cutting. Lynn looked up toward the shed again just in time to see CJ's buddies climbing into their truck. CJ waved good bye and then went to close up the wood shed door. Lynn looked around at the old place and smiled. She never thought she would want to live here, so far away from everyone and so near a cemetery that held no one she knew. Lynn put her feet up on the railing that edged the porch. Her legs were tired and her ankles were slightly swollen, but she was happy and CJ looked contented as he strolled toward the cabin.

He could not wait to see Pa Bowers and reassure him that everything would be just fine. CJ was shaking his head slowly from side to side as he stepped up onto the porch.

"This has been an amazing day, my love."

"Yes, it has," answered Lynn. CJ slid behind his wife and sat in the rocker next to her. Lynn passed her half of glass of iced tea to CJ and she then put her head back and closed her eyes to relax. He sipped at the iced tea and was watching the sun as it drifted ever so slowly over the trees. What a breathtaking sunset to end the day. He noticed how tired Lynn was and that her ankles were slightly swollen. He thought on the next trip into town they had better get her a more supportive pair of shoes. She had been going non-stop and the terrain up in the mountains was not made for little canvas sneakers. He also noticed that Lynn was getting a pot belly. He thought this would never have happened if they were back home. She would be watching everything she ate and fast food would be out of the question. He liked her a little rounder - he would like her any way she was. She was his world.

CJ finished the iced tea then he nudged Lynn, who had drifted off for a short time.

"It's time to get inside babe, and get some shuteye. We have another busy day tomorrow."

"You're right," she replied, "and thank you for the wonderful job you guys did with the fridge and generator, and a special thanks for carrying in all those bags of groceries."

"You're welcome and we're even. You bought them all and made a nice meal for all of us, and the guys really had a good time."

"Good, the day is done and so are we."

CJ agreed. As the two of them lay in bed, CJ told Lynn that in the morning he would check out the shower shed that was just several feet from the cabin. He hoped he could divert the water supply back to it and they could shower before going to town. He'd looked it over earlier and he didn't think it would take much to fix it. The most time consuming part would be removing the wildlife out of it. The buggies move in and they don't like to leave.

Lynn was out and CJ knew it. Even though the sun was set for the night and the moon was high in the sky, it was as though the lights were on all over the cabin. It was bright and clean and now with Lynn there and Sheridan on his way back, it was complete. Yes, it was home.

Bright and early next morning, while Lynn slept, CJ was up and out working on the shower. It must not have been unused too long by Sheridan because it took little work returning the water from one of the springs back into a catcher on the top of the shed. The catcher would hold the water for the sun to warm, then by slowly pulling the rope a small hole opens in the bottom of the catcher and down comes warm water. It's all gravity fed and as you use the warm water it's gradually replaced by the spring water so it will get colder in time. Showers have to be thought out and the warm water used frugally or your rinse water may be chillier than you would like.

CJ continued to clean out the insects; he even sprayed the shed with a disinfectant spray. When Lynn woke he would show her the shower and give her first dibs on the warm water in the catcher. With that task completed, he walked back down to the cabin and started up the cook stove so he could make coffee and hot water for tea. As the stove snapped and crackled as it consumed the kindling, he checked the coldness of the refrigerator and freezer. They were working perfectly and the generator was really easy on the gas.

Great, Lynn would be happy this morning--the sun was promising another warm beautiful day, everything was working well, and she could have a much wanted shower. They could visit with Sheridan later. This would be the first time for he and Lynn to meet. CJ knew they would like each other, after all, he loved both of them and they loved him so it sounded like it would be a mutual admiration threesome.

"Hey, good morning, Babe, how did you sleep?"

"I feel good and refreshed. How about you, CJ? How long have you been up?"

"Just long enough to fix and clean the shower shed and to bring the cook stove up to frying heat. The generator and the refrigerator are doing a great job, and the Lord blessed us with another warm bright day. I'd say we're doing ok," and he gave Lynn a hug and a kiss.

"I agree and I'm starved. Let me start with some breakfast sausages and eggs."

"While you do that I'll empty out the springhouse and put the items in the fridge."

"Sounds like a plan," said Lynn, as she loaded sausage links into a frying pan.

CJ entered the springhouse and bent down to watch the frogs jump into the water. He loaded his arms with the items that the spring water had kept cold and fresh. This would probably be the last time they used this liquid fridge, but CJ had vowed to keep it clean and ready to go just in case.

With his arms full and wet from the water, CJ started back to the cabin. Unable to open the door with his arms full he tapped his shoe against the door frame. Lynn, hearing this, laid down her spatula and opened the door. She followed him to the refrigerator and helped to remove items from his arms and place them in a more modern version of cold storage.

"Sit down, my mountain man, I've got a morning feast for you."

CJ sat at the table and could not believe his eyes when Lynn placed plate after plate on the table.

"Who is going to eat all of this, babe?"

"Aren't you hungry?"

"Yes, but I only have one stomach, honest. It looks great, but we could feed four hungry men."

"I'm really hungry and it didn't seem like much when I was cooking it. I'm really sorry," she said, and her eyes started to fill up with tears.

"Don't cry about it, babe, it's only food. What we can't eat now we will later."

"I guess my eyes were bigger then your belly."

"I think so, too," and they both laughed and ate.

The whole situation left an uneasy feeling in CJ. Not the fact that it seemed like she over cooked, but that it brought her to tears when he questioned it. Well, he thought all their nerves were a little on the raw side considering what they had been through and the decisions they had to make.

CJ grabbed another cup of coffee and headed to the sitting room to relax and wait for Lynn to finish her meal. Neither one of them spoke, they were absorbed in their own thoughts and actions. Lynn finally declared she was done with breakfast.

"Good," said CJ, "now would you like to try out the shower? It's pretty self-explanatory once you get in."

"That sounds great."

"Well, go ahead and I'll clean up the dishes and put things away."

"Are you sure, CJ?"

"Yeah, I'm sure. I can wash dishes, honest."

"OK, there's hot water on the stove."

Lynn took off for the bedroom for clean clothes and a wash cloth and towel as CJ headed toward the table to put away left over food and fruit. He could not believe how little was left. Maybe one scrambled egg, one half slice of pan toasted bread, and a few chunks of melon mixed with two slices of banana. Lynn was starved and CJ even ate more then he usually would have so her feelings were not hurt.

As he was surveying the mess to clean up, Lynn scampered through the kitchen and out the door on her way to a most wanted shower.

"Be frugal with the warm water or it will turn cold fast," yelled CJ.

The slamming of the shower shed door was witness that Lynn was accepting of the way it was cleaned. CJ put the fruit into a small dish with a snap top on it and threw away the egg and toast. With good hot dishwater in the dishpan clean up was on its way.

Lynn entered the kitchen at the same time her mountain man was placing the last plate onto its stack in the cupboard.

"You do good work, my man. The shower was wonderful, I just have to get a better sense of timing with the water flow. I really feel clean and refreshed and I don't smell like a bear anymore."

They both laughed and hugged. The kitchen was in good shape, too. The dishes were done, the table was clean, and the dish towel was hung to dry.

"Are you going to shower now, CJ?"

"No, I think I'm going to wait for the sun to take the chill off the spring water first. Did you have something you wanted me to do while I wait?"

"Not right now. I'm going to get some city clothes laid out for us for our trip to town later."

She looked at him and smiled impishly. "I have some clothes to sort out and put away in the closet and dresser, too, so I'll be tied up in there for awhile."

"Alright. I'm going to clean the guns over the fireplace so when Sheridan comes home he'll see how much respect we have for him and his home."

"Oh, ok," said Lynn on her way down the hall. But under her breath she said, "You mean, our home."

Lynn continued into the master bedroom and CJ went into a small closet along side of the fireplace that had always held the gun cleaning equipment. He was so at home there he could remember where almost everything was kept or put.

"I guess I'm more of a Bowers than I thought I was," he said to himself. "When I was a kid and I was here visiting through the summers I was taught where things were. Ma and Pa Bowers said they were not here to wait on my needs and wants, they had their chores to do just like all us boys had. So best learn were things are so you can help yourself, because you're kin as far as we are concerned. We share with our kin all we have."

CJ removed the cleaning rod and oily rags from the closet and a tear ran down his face.

"Yep," he said, "I'm proud to be kin."

As if he was holding a baby, CJ removed and cleaned each of the five guns that were on the wooden gun rack over the fireplace. He carefully laid down each gun and polished the next. Once he had the guns gleaming inside and out with a new fine coat of oil, he cleaned off the gun rack itself and replaced the guns one by one. He reminisced times he could recall when he would see each gun's owner holding or shooting his weapon. He missed them all so. He replaced the cleaning equipment back to its proper place in the side closet, then he stepped back and admired how beautiful the guns and the rack looked. Making Pa proud of you or your actions meant a lot back then and it would be the same today.

The corner clock struck 12 noon. Where did the time go and CJ almost forgot to wind the clock again. Things were different up here but he would not mind the differences. He started down the hall to the bedroom to get a washcloth and towel. As he came out to go to the shower, he noted that Lynn must have finished her work and had fallen asleep in the bright daylight. She was so pretty, he thought, and she had a glow about her. Mountain living must agree with her because she beamed. He let her sleep while he showered, and taking that time to clean the guns gave the sun time for its rays of heat to dance in the shower catcher and warm the water.

God was good and CJ sang a few old time church songs as he bathed. With his towel wrapped around him, out of the shower shed he came. He passed by the clothes line on his way back to the cabin were he hung his wash cloth up to dry by Lynn's cloth and towel. Then he headed toward the cabin's back door where he would wake Lynn so they could dress and head for town to see Sheridan.

Lynn was already up and nicely dressed. She was putting on some lip gloss and combing back her hair so she could style it in a way that it would cover her dark roots. When they got to town she would visit a pharmacy and get pads and hair dye that would bring her own color back again. No more blonde, it was too much trouble and she was finally comfortable with the way she was.

Lynn had laid out clothes for CJ, too. As he dried off, she took his towel so he could finish dressing.

"I'll meet you out by the SUV," she said. "I'm going to check the kitchen stove and hang up your towel to dry. See you in a little," she said, as she walked toward the kitchen.

CJ dressed as Lynn followed through on her word. She hung the towel and then headed toward the SUV. Realizing that CJ was still inside, she stepped off the path to the SUV and headed toward the cemetery. It was so beautiful, yet so foreboding; even with the sun fully out, the air was colder inside of the gate. She carefully walked from cross to cross reading dates and epitaphs. To think these people walked where she was walking now was a little unnerving, but she did nothing to them so she had nothing to fear from them.

It made her wonder about her own roots. She loved her mother and father dearly and she was an only child. All she had left was a great aunt and a dear friend with whom she had grown up. But they were both back in Romania. It had been a long time since she had received or sent letters to either of them. When she and CJ called his folks tonight she would have the mail sent here to Raven Hill. Then she would splurge on a phone call to Romania telling her kin where to write to. It would be fun updating them on her new lifestyle. CJ was coming out of the cabin at the same time Lynn was bending down to read Robert Jake's epitaph. It was also the same time a rogue raven was screaming in flight over the cemetery.

CJ yelled to Lynn to run to him as he was running toward her. Lynn was totally confused and caught off guard by his reaction to the bird and her being under it as it flew through the branches of the oak tree, over her and the grave of Robert Jake.

CJ dashed through the gate and held her tightly.

"What…what is it, CJ? Are you afraid of birds or was it something else?"

"Are you ok, honey?"

"Yes, of course, I was just reading the grave stones while I waited for you to get ready. What scared you so, CJ?"

"Nothing, baby, the raven caught me off guard when it screamed. I, I, uh, thought it was you screaming."

"Why would I be screaming?"

"I don't know, maybe you got into bees or saw a snake. I'm sorry for being so protective of you, Lynn. I just love you so and you never know what birds and animals will do, especially up here in the mountains."

"What?" said Lynn in disbelief.

"Nothing. Let's go, babe. It's going to be a ride there and back. I left a night light on in the sitting room."

"That's fine, CJ, lets go."

The ride down the mountain was time consuming, but the beauty of the trees and a glimpse of deer and fox around every tree made it hard not to enjoy the sights even though you had to keep your eye on the ruts and grooves.

After safely reaching town, they headed toward the highway that would take them to the hospital where Sheridan was recouping. Just a few more turns and --- "Oh my goodness," said CJ.

Lynn could not believe her eyes either. There was mass media and mass confusion. News vans were everywhere and people were looking up and pointing at the south side of the hospital. There were blackbirds suspended from every sill and wire that was either on or entering into the hospital. CJ stopped and watched in awe.

"Why are they there, CJ, the birds, why are they there?"

"I'm not sure, babe."

"It's scary," said Lynn.

"Yeah, it is."

"Why don't they chase them away?"

"Dr. Miles said they tried to no avail."

"You knew about this?"

"Only from what the doctor said. Who could have imagined this?"

A policeman walked up to the SUV and asked why they were there.

"We are here to see a loved one under Dr. Miles' care."

"OK," he said, "let this SUV through."

CJ drove very slowly through the crowds of officials and sightseers. While looking for a place to park, an officer leaned toward the SUV and told CJ not to rev his engine or blow his horn. No one was sure what the effect on the birds would be, but they seemed to just quietly sit there. CJ was fortunate to park fairly close to the main entrances. He closed the windows as Lynn grabbed her purse.

"Wait until I come around to get you, Lynn. Then together we'll go in."

"Don't slam your door, CJ."

"I won't."

CJ opened the door slowly and slid out of the SUV. He knew the birds were watching everything. He proceeded to go around the vehicle and open Lynn's door slowly and quietly letting her slide out, grabbing his arm. Everyone was quietly and intently watching the birds. Cameras were running their new takes and it was hard to believe that many people could be so quiet.

CJ and Lynn started to make their way into the hospital when all of a sudden the ravens started screaming and flying in circles above them. They were terrified and so were the others. The sound was shrill and deafening. The flapping of that many wings was like being in a wind tunnel. CJ and Lynn ran for their lives into the foyer and some of the birds crashed into the door glass, breaking their necks. The others flew around and then returned to the side of the building as though nothing happened. Everyone was asking CJ and Lynn what they did to upset the birds.

"Nothing," they replied.

"Then what happened out there that did it?"

"We don't know, we're asking ourselves the same question," said Lynn.

"Please people, go on about your business and leave this man and his wife alone. No one did anything, it's just a quirk in the bird kingdom. Hi, CJ and Lynn."

"We're glad to see you, Dr. Miles."

"I feel the same, and I think you will be glad you came today. Shall we go see Mr. Bowers? This way to the elevator."

They entered and the doctor pushed the button for floor 3. Up they went, still shaken but feeling more secure with the brick walls between them and the birds.

"Here we are, room 312. It's a private room so you won't be disturbed. My office is just around the corner. Please see me before you leave. I'll be catching up on paperwork so just walk in."

"Ok, and thanks again."

Dr. Miles walked away and left CJ and Lynn outside Sheridan's room, which was located on the north side of the building.

"Wait, CJ, before we go in, why don't you go first and see if he's up to meeting me. It will be awkward for both of us, especially if he's not ready or ashamed of his health problems, you know?"

"Wait here for me, there's a chair over there for you to sit in."

"I'll be right here waiting, take your time."

CJ entered the room and Sheridan started to laugh and cry at the same time. He waved his arms and CJ rushed to hug him.

"Oh, Pa, I'm so glad you're feeling better and on the road to recovery. I've been so worried about you."

Sheridan pointed to himself and then at CJ; the feeling was mutual. Sheridan had a letter board so he could express himself. He pointed to the letters spelling, "want to go home, miss mountain."

"I know how you feel, Pa."

"Cannot take care of self now. Want to go home, son."

CJ and Sheridan held on to each other and cried.

"Pa, listen to me. I think I can take you home if you will compromise with me."

Sheridan shook his head indicating that he would. "Yes," he nodded over and over again.

"First you must be well enough to travel back, and that may be by helicopter, the same way you got here."

It was unknown by Sheridan how he'd gotten to the hospital, he was unconscious when it all took place. He did not want to travel by air, but his want to go home was greater than his fear of the helicopter.

"Donnie and his pa plus me and my wife, Lynn, cleaned up the cabin, sheds and grounds up on Raven Hill. Lynn and I are willing to live up there with you and care for you if it's what you want. The other choice would be to find you a place where you could receive good care and meals and we could visit with you."

Sheridan was overwhelmed, but in a good way.

"Pa, would you like to meet Lynn? She's outside the door and she is more than willing to help." Sheridan pulled his blanket closer to his chest and shook his head yes. CJ opened the door and motioned for Lynn to come in. She was a little hesitant, but smiled and strolled in.

"Hi, Mr. Bowers, I'm CJ's wife, Lynn. I'm so glad you're on the road to recovery. I truly want to help. The question is, am I also welcomed by you to live up on Raven Hill? I don't want to be separated from my husband, and you guys will need a woman's touch."

Sheridan picked up his word board and spelled out "Glad to know you, Lynn. Please take me home, you're welcome Child." They all looked at each other and the tears flowed down their cheeks.

"Good," said Lynn, "and I make a mean apple pie."

She excused herself from the room saying she needed to go for a walk. That she did, she walked toward Dr. Miles' office, feeling a little faint and queasy. Lynn tapped on the door and walked in announcing herself.

"Come in, Lynn, I'm here."

As soon as she cleared the door she sat down. Dr. Miles came out to see where she was, and found her sitting in a chair, shaken and pale.

"What's the matter Lynn, is Sheridan ok?"

"Yes, he is more than fine, and happy to be able to return to Raven Hill in time with us caring for him. It went too easily, and I think it shocked me or something, Doctor. I didn't feel well for the last four months, but then things changed last week and I felt great. The nausea stopped and then I was able to eat again. Now I'm always starved and I noticed my ankles are slightly swollen, too."

"I think you came to the right place, Lynn. Let me call a colleague to examine you, because your problem is probably outside of my practice."

"Should I worry, Dr. Miles?"

"No need to worry."

He picked up the phone and the loud speaker sang out, "Dr. Adams, please call Dr. Miles office."

Within seconds his phone rang and he asked the person on the other end of the phone to please come to his office, he thought he had need of their expertise. A short time later a small built woman walked in and flashed a big smile at the two of them.

"Hi, I'm Dr. Adams, may I examine you?"

"Yes. I'm Lynn Rolley and I think I'm scared."

"Don't worry, Lynn, you'll be fine."

"I'm going to occupy CJ and Sheridan, and you two ladies please feel free to use my examining room."

"Here, Lynn," said Dr Adams, "slip off your clothes and we'll start with a physical."

Dr. Miles slipped out the door and down the hall to room 312. Lynn went into the inner room which held an exam table. There she took off her clothes and placed a thin gown on. Next she sat on the table, thinking how glad she was that she showered that morning and how thankful she was that Dr. Adams would check her out while she was there.

"I'm ready," Lynn called out.

"We'll be right in, Lynn."

The door opened and the doctor and a nurse walked in. As Dr. Adams gave Lynn a complete physical, the nurse was busy preparing for Lynn's internal examine.

"Well, Lynn, I think I know why you feel the way you do, but let's do a pelvic exam first before I diagnose you."

Lynn hated this part, but she did feel more comfortable with a woman doctor.

"Just as I thought," said Dr. Adams, with a smile on her face.

"What wrong, Doctor, is it life threatening?"

"Well, tender breasts, weight gain, nausea, slight dizziness, plus swollen ankles, and this last exam all add up to you're about 4 months pregnant. I still need some blood, but I think you're just fine, Mom. Congratulations, you're going to have a baby."

The doctor and nurse left the room so Lynn could get dressed. Lynn was in shock. It was what they always wanted. The timing was not good, but they were going to have a child. Oh, how wonderful. How would CJ feel, and what about Sheridan's feeling? Who cares, we are having a baby and it will be brought up living on Raven Hill. Now to find the right time to tell CJ.

Chapter 10

As she walked back to Sheridan's room, the two doctors were talking in the hall. Dr. Miles smiled and offered his congratulations.

"You two are really going to have your hands full, but I'm sure you can handle it all well."

"Thank you," said Lynn. "I'm going to tell CJ at dinner tonight."

Dr. Adams gave Lynn her card and phone number with an appointment to return for a check up in one month if she did not hear from them. By then the blood report would be done and it would be time for a sonogram.

Lynn tapped on Sheridan's door and stepped in quietly. He and CJ had been enjoying each other's company. As Lynn walked in Sheridan glanced her way and smiled. Lynn thought he looked tired and older then his years, although he was no kid. He was well into his seventies.

CJ looked at Lynn inquisitively, wondering were she had been. Lynn just smiled and watched Sheridan as he pointed to letters on the board.

"Glad you moved to Raven Hill. I will work hard to get well and come home."

CJ spoke to Sheridan calmly reminding him the doctor said slow and easy. He had been through a lot and his body needed care and rest to get stronger. Sheridan nodded his head in agreement.

Dr. Miles said, "Maybe in a few weeks, by then you will be receiving speech therapy and physical therapy, so you will be able to talk and walk again in time."

Again Sheridan nodded his head. He totally understood what was being said and he realized that it was for his own good.

"We'll come back every few days to see you again, Pa. The doctor said we can't stay long and tire you out. Donnie and his dad will be here tomorrow to visit. Is there anything you need or want?"

Again Pa grabbed the board and signed out "glasses and Bible."

"I'll bring them next time."

Pa pointed out "ok" and "thank you, son." Lynn said good-bye and stepped out of the room so CJ was free to hug his mountain father goodbye, then he joined her in the hall.

"Where were you, Lynn?" CJ asked. "I was getting concerned, then Dr. Miles came in and said you were talking to some women."

"He was right. I was fine, let's get out of here. Don't forget we must call your mom and dad tonight about our house. Maybe your mom can have our mail sent to us up on Raven Hill."

"Are you kidding? It will go to Serpentine Gulch and we'll have to go get it once a week."

The two of them entered the elevator and pushed the lobby button. CJ told Lynn that Sheridan approved of her, which would make living together much more sociable. Lynn had to admit he was more like a regular man then she thought he would be.

"I expected him to be more primitive I guess," she told CJ. "With living on the mountain and not really socializing much with others, I thought he would grunt and be unresponsive to me. By the time he can come home maybe we will have some kind of friendship to bond us."

"I think the two of you are going to be fine together. I hope he gets his voice back soon so he can tell us some more Bowers history. Believe me, he can really weave a tale."

As they exited the lobby elevator, they could see a lot of the crowd had dispersed. There were a lot less cars in the parking lot, maybe because it was late in the afternoon and most of the news vans were gone. But it was obvious the birds were still on the south wall and there was still a number of spectators watching them.

CJ told Lynn to wait at the door and he would drive over to her, but she, being a liberated woman who was not going to let her hubby face the birds alone, said "No, we do this together."

They locked hands and walked out the double doors straight to the SUV. Several ravens made a pass at CJ trying to peck him on the head, but none approached Lynn. She waved her purse at them and said "shoo" and "get away." This action seemed to cause them to fly back up to the wires above them and just cackle as the SUV drove out of the parking lot and headed back home.

"What was that all about?" asked CJ. "Why did they attack me and not bother with you?"

"It's pretty obvious." she said. "You're taller then I am and easier to hit."

"Well, maybe. You were surely brave, baby, chasing them off me. It was like they wanted to please you so they left."

"Oh, sure, CJ, like I have any power over birds."

Lynn could see that the bird attack really upset CJ, so she thought that she would change the subject.

"I really enjoyed meeting Sheridan. I was surprised that he was so open to me and the fact that we would all be living together."

CJ heard her but did not respond, so she went on to ask if he had any idea how long it would until Sheridan might be able to come home.

"Well, Dr. Miles thought that maybe within a month, if there were no more setbacks."

"A month, huh."

"Why," asked CJ, "what are you thinking?"

"Oh, nothing we can't talk about over dinner. Why don't we stop at that nice restaurant that we took the guys to the other night. It will be dark when we return to Raven Hill no matter if we stop or not."

"Well, I guess we could, and while we're waiting for our meal we could call Mom and Dad and let them know what's going on. We can also ask if they would help us get the house ready to rent."

"Good, by the time we get to the restaurant I will be starved again," stated Lynn.

"Your appetite has become unbelievable."

"Yeah, I guess this mountain air agrees with me."

CJ pulled into the parking lot of the restaurant. There were not too many customers dining that night, so they were able to park right in front. They both slid out of the SUV and closed the doors. CJ told Lynn that before he could eat he needed to take a walk, so please go ahead and order him a cup of coffee. He would find their table when he returned.

They walked in and CJ took off down the hall to the men's room while Lynn waited to be seated by the hostess.

"Hi," said the hostess, "I remember you from the other night."

"Yes, we thoroughly enjoyed our meals so we thought we'd return."

The hostess led Lynn toward a table near where several diners were already seated. Asked if that was agreeable, Lynn responded that she'd like to have a corner table away from others because she and her husband had some private matters to talk about as they dined.

"Sure, I can do that. How about back there," pointing to a cozy table back on the left side of the room away from everyone. She sat Lynn and took her drink order with the promise that a waitress would be there shortly.

"Thank you very much for accommodating us," Lynn said.

"No problem. Now you enjoy and take all the time you need to dine and talk."

As the hostess was leaving the table, CJ was walking down the aisle looking for Lynn.

"Wow, why so far back in the corner, Lynn?"

"It's nice and private so you can talk to Mom and Dad, but first I can't wait to tell you something and I hope you're alright with it."

At that time a waitress was placing one hot coffee and one hot tea on the table as ordered.

"Do you know what you want to order?" she asked.

CJ did not have to look at the menu, he wanted a large steak, baked potato and corn for his veggie. Lynn really wanted to talk more than eat, but eating was good, too.

"I'll have the roast chicken platter."

"Fine, I'll bring your salads out right away. What kind of dressing to you want with them?"

They both answered ranch on the side.

"I'll be right back," and away she walked.

Before they could start the conversation up again, the salads were delivered with ranch on the side. Each prepared their drink and salad, then paused to say grace. They ate quietly, savoring their salad and beverages. The waitress showing up had broken Lynn's momentum. She would have to regroup her thoughts on announcing her pregnancy. With their first course over they sipped at their hot drinks and relaxed.

"What did you want to say before our drinks and salad were delivered?" asked CJ.

"If you could have anything that would make you happy, what would you want?"

"Sheridan to be alright and back home."

"Besides that, what?"

"For the house to be rented and totally peaceful times up on Raven Hill."

"Yeah, me too. But think hard, CJ, before all this happened what was one thing you really wanted? We really wanted."

"To hit the lottery, retire, and travel."

Lynn was going to say more until the waitress announced CJ's steak platter and her chicken platter were in her hands and she was now placing them on the table for their approval.

"Thank you," said Lynn. "Could I ask a favor of you, please?"

"Yes, what is it?"

"May we both have refills on our drinks and extra napkins, then if we need anything else we'll ask for it. We have some important business to discuss."

"Sure, OK."

She returned with the items Lynn asked for then quietly walked away.

"What was that about, Lynn?" asked CJ.

"I want to be able to relax, eat, and talk uninterrupted." CJ dived into his steak as Lynn just watched. Slowly she started to pick at her meal and think to herself about CJ's answers to her questions. Before all this happened the two of them spoke often about having a child to love and rear. Now what had changed, if it did?

"Lynn, maybe it would be best for you to make an appointment with Dr. Miles, so when we visit with Sheridan you can be checked over."

"Why would you say that?" she asked.

"Well, you just don't seem to always be yourself at times. Usually you're starving and now you sit there picking at you meal and you seem to be tense, or something. And I'm worried about you and your health. You know, when Sheridan comes home, for awhile it will probably be even more stressful.

"CJ, I'm pregnant," said Lynn but, CJ yammered on. "CJ, I'm pregnant and Dr. Miles and Dr. Adams know it, too. I'm 4 months along."

There was dead silence and CJ never took his eyes from his plate.

"Pregnant," he said.

"Yes, Papa, definitely with child and healthy. Are you happy CJ? Aren't you amazed we did it?"

"Yes, I'm thrilled and in shock and now I'm going to change our plans."

"From what to what?" asked Lynn.

"We are going back home to live and I will find Sheridan a place to reside where he can get the best of all he needs."

"Oh, no, I don't want that. I want to stay and live on Raven Hill. That's where we all belong: Sheridan, you, me, and our future child. Please let's stay, CJ."

"Sheridan will be a lot of work and so will a baby. I can't do it all and you will be in no shape to do it either."

"If I can come up with a plan for all of this to work out then please, will you reconsider?"

"Reconsider what, that you are my love and my first priority, you and our child? You have no medical care up there. Who will deliver the baby? Not me, babe. Diapers, maybe. Hello, world, not my thing."

"Please, we have time to think about it and then choose."

The whole scenario hit CJ and he grabbed Lynn and hugged her with joy, love, amazement and trepidation. They laughed and showed amusement about the timing of the pregnancy.

"CJ, as soon as we didn't try so hard and gave it no thought we got blessed. I can't wait to tell Mom and Dad and everyone. I wonder how Sheridan will feel about this?"

"Well, he'll either love having a set of little feet around or he'll hate a repetition of family life dramas after all this time. It's his choice, we stay or he's institutionalized."

They finished their meals and even had dessert before they headed back up the mountain. CJ left a nice tip for the waitress for her politely obliging with Lynn's request of privacy during their meal.

Once in the SUV, CJ took out his cell phone and called home. Mom answered and was so glad to hear from them. Between Lynn and CJ, Mom and Dad were updated on Sheridan and the possibility of their staying up on Raven Hill to care for him. They also talked about renting their house out for a time until they knew what the future would hold. CJ explained to his Dad that Mr. Bowers had willed CJ Raven Hill upon his death. He said he had seen the will and it was legal and binding. CJ was overwhelmed to think that he could be so loved that Sheridan made that decision, and after all this time, too.

They all agreed there was nothing that could not be taken care of as far as CJ and Lynn relocating to Serpentine Gulch. They would surely miss them, but vacationing on Raven Hill would be awesome. It had been years since CJ's mother and father had been there and that was only twice. CJ's grandparents could and would visit frequently, after all they lived at the bottom of the mountain.

CJ finally had his mom and dad on two separate phones so they could have a three way conversation. He then told them that Lynn wanted to speak to them also. Lynn started with the normal "I miss you both," which was the truth, she loved them dearly. She then said she loved Raven Hill especially because it was primitive and peacefully quiet. She could understand why CJ loved it so up there when he was a child. She said she hoped that their grandchild would be happy growing up there also.

Mom cried out, "You're pregnant, aren't you dear?"

"Yes, I'm 4 months and we are thrilled."

"Will you be alright up there with so much responsibility and so little medical care?"

"I think so. CJ is a little uneasy right now, but I'm healthy and happy and the doctors will have input into our final decision. We have time and after all, babies came into this world without doctors before, Mom."

"That's true. CJ's dad was delivered at home in Serpentine Gulch by a midwife who lived in town, and he and his mom were fine. We will help however we can, kids. Pray on it, and plan accordingly."

"We are so happy for all of us," Dad said.

After that, they exchanged good byes and Mom and Dad would deal with the renting of the house. They would all stay in touch. Love would conquer all, they agreed.

On the way back up the mountain CJ and Lynn thought about names and how to arrange which bedroom for who. If Sheridan was understanding and wanting of the baby, Lynn was going to ask if she could use the baby furniture that was stored out in one of the sheds. She was also going to push her luck and ask about the beautiful baby clothes and blankets that she saw in the hope chest at the bottom of the master bed. She was sure that Mrs. Bowers would love for CJ's first child to be able to get some good out of them. They were made with so much love.

She really wanted to sort through them and select at least a couple of items, if not all. CJ figured if Sheridan didn't mind another person around he probably would not mind sharing his children's furniture or clothing with his adopted new born kin. Mrs. Bowers would have been honored to let Lynn bundle her little one in her son's coverings.

They made it up the hill in the dark and could see that the night light was still on, so CJ knew the generator was still going strong. They parked the SUV and headed directly for bed. Tomorrow would mark the first day of officially being pregnant. It would be a wonderful day, even if it rained or snowed or did whatever. It would not change the fact that it was not just CJ and Lynn anymore, it was Mommy and Daddy to be, as of February.

Each slept so peacefully and so relaxed, it had become the norm ever since they moved to Raven Hill. They both awoke to the sound of the birds chirping and the rays of the sun peeking into their bedroom window. Each reached for the other, with smiles that creased from ear to ear. It was true and wanted. They were going to be parents. No matter what else happened, they would be holding their bundle of joy in February.

They hugged and kissed and sighed with great feelings of contentment. Lynn lingered in bed for a few minutes longer than C.J. She heard the back door open and close as she laid there imagining everything good about the life she was carrying in her. Again the back door opened and closed. That was it, time to rise and shine. She also was fully aware that her bladder was not as large as she thought it to be.

She got up from the bed and wrapped her robe around her, the mornings were pretty chilly now. The night air would drop some and stay that way until the sun was well over head. Fall was here.

Lynn passed CJ in the kitchen where he was stoking the stove for hot water and heat enough to fry up some pancakes. She went out the back door and headed for the privy. The walk was a little bit of a hike considering the privy was the farthest building from the house. As she walked along she was really amazed at how many leaves had started to change color. There had been so much going on that observing the leaves never figured into their schedules.

Lynn returned to the cabin and sat down at the table. CJ had the frying pan out and was mixing up one of those pancake containers that you only add water to and fry. He was happy and as he danced around her at the table he sang Rockabye Baby. Lynn smiled at him and tapped her belly lovingly, hoping that the baby would feel her comforting touch.

Breakfast was filling and tasty. CJ headed outside to check the gas level in the generator and maybe cut some more wood. Lynn got dressed and cleaned up the breakfast dishes. She decided to walk outside and enjoy the last of summer while it was still there. By the time she got outside, she could hear and see CJ working on the wood supply. There was a lot cut and stored, but winters can be long and cold up in the mountains, so better too much than not enough.

She walked to the top of the hill above the cabin and cemetery where the ground seemed to level off at one end. It was the place where the helicopter landed to take Sheridan to the hospital. It was so pretty and so still. On the other side of the clearing the mountain continued up and across a ravine that divided Raven Hill from another large rock formation. It was so private that the only way to get there was by the coming up the cattle trail from town or flying by helicopter to the landing above the cemetery.

Lynn headed back to the main part of the yard to watch CJ and just snoop around. She wanted to see the baby furniture in the shed and maybe dust it off and wash it. She could clean up the pieces she wanted to use and then wait for Sheridan's approval to revarnish or paint them.

Chapter 11

S everal weeks had passed, and between Donnie and his pa, and CJ and Lynn, Sheridan was never long without visitors. He seemed to be doing well, and his therapy was well tolerated. Lynn and CJ had learned how to continue his therapy after he was back home. He had no restrictions on food or drink, so that was great. Sheridan himself was eager to return to Raven Hill. Dr. Miles thought it may be best to give it two more weeks before the air trip home.

Lynn and CJ were amazed that every time they went to visit Sheridan, the birds were still there and still unwilling to leave. The media had stopped spending so much time there anymore. It was old news without any changes. Even the locals ignored the situation, only commenting on the amount of bird waste that daily had to be hosed down and the cost of sanitizing the area.

Today CJ and Lynn had decided to tell Sheridan about the baby. If he was upset about it there was still time to relocate him somewhere that he would receive proper care and therapy. Lynn had grown close to Sheridan the past month. They seemed to be quite comfortable in each other's presence. CJ hoped things would work out so they would be friends and it looked like he might get his wish. Lynn thought that it would be easier for Sheridan to make his wishes known if CJ was not in the room when she told him about the baby. CJ hemmed and hawed, but agreed to get lost for 10 minutes so the announcement and reaction could occur.

CJ left the room, just as Lynn was finishing up giving Sheridan a foot rub. He loved the way it felt and it was relaxing for him. He was also surprised that Lynn would want to rub and lotion his feet. It started off a little embarrassing for him but it was part of his physical therapy. Lynn had no qualms about it so all went well. Lynn put socks on Sheridan's feet and returned his foot lotion to his drawer.

"Sheridan," she said as she walked toward the sink to wash her hands, "I want to tell you something that I hope makes you happy. It's important to CJ and me that you tell us your true feeling on this matter."

Sheridan's mind raced trying to second guess the matter at hand. Lynn looked at Sheridan and he nodded yes.

"I'm going to have a baby in February. It was not a planned pregnancy, but it was a most wanted one. I'm fine and healthy and the baby will not take away from us caring for you at home, but it's your home and your decision if you can tolerate the sound and confusion of having a new born up on Raven Hill. If not, then…"

Lynn never got another word out. Sheridan was waving his hands and laughing. His words were coming back slowly and he was able to say, "Good, good, good."

He and Lynn were hugging as CJ walked into the room. Again Sheridan waved his hands and said, "Good."

He grabbed his spelling board and pointed to letters spelling, "Use baby clothes in footlocker and furniture in shed if you want. Ma would want you to. Good thing new generation."

CJ and Lynn were elated by his reactions to the baby. When everyone was composed again, Lynn asked Sheridan if the child in time could call him Great Pa. His eyes filled up as he looked at CJ and nodded yes. With everyone happy and looking forward with great expectation of blessings to come, it was a good time to leave the hospital so Sheridan could rest and it was a good time to start back home.

Lynn and CJ said farewells to Sheridan and exited his room. They headed toward the elevator with smiles plastered to their faces and a lightness in their hearts they had not felt in sometime whenever they visited or talked about Sheridan Bowers. Things were changing now and life was looking better with each passing day.

The two of them swiftly and cautiously exited the main lobby doors and headed directly for the SUV. There were still some bird watchers, but the birds out numbered the people and the birds did nothing out of the norm.

The ride back to Serpentine Gulch was light and happy. It seemed liked everyone's dreams were coming true. Sheridan would be coming home by the end of October and a new little person would be making its debut the first week of February. CJ now realized that his cloud of confusion and problems really had a silver lining, he just had to get through the dilemmas that surrounded the lining and its rewards.

The two decided to stop at a supermart and pick up a few items. Lynn would finally get her hair dye and be able to return her hair to a shade closer to her own. CJ wanted to check out varnishes so he could redo the baby furniture. He did not want Lynn working with varnish or paint. They also got some milk, more bread for the freezer, and a bag of chocolate candy bars that Lynn slipped onto the counter at check out. They would now be on their way back to Raven Hill and they probably would not be going to the hospital again. The next time they saw Sheridan, it would be by helicopter.

The trees were so beautiful, the colors were so vivid, and each leaf was perfectly color coordinated with its tree. Lynn slipped on her sweater, for the days were shorter and cooler. She was more aware of the fall, maybe because she was pregnant or maybe because it was just colder living under all these trees.

It was always a wonderful feeling when the SUV came over the last part of the mountain trail. There it was, the cabin and the sheds, their home sweet home in front of them. It seemed like the place was always waiting for their return. Once the SUV was parked, Lynn headed toward the cabin door to start up the stove and heat up some soup to go along with the sandwiches she would make. CJ brought in the items they had purchased and placed them on the table. He was in the process of emptying the bag when his cell phone rang.

"Hello," he answered as he placed the phone to his ear. Lynn stopped to look and hear.

"Oh, hi Dad, what's up?"

Lynn went back to the sandwich making and CJ continued talking to his father.

"Wow, Dad, that's great. Was it hard for you and Mom to scout through the house and remove our personal items and papers? I'm sorry to lay it on you both, but we sure do thank you for your love and help.

"Oh, he's doing fine, and should be home by airlift the end of October. Lynn's got his room all set up, she has the whole cabin clean and homey and comfortable."

As the two men spoke, Lynn got water for hot drinks and dishes started on the stove. The soup was slowly warming and the whole cabin was smelling so good. The colder weather had a way of making everything that was cooked cause the whole cabin to smell inviting and cozy.

"Sounds like you and Mom have all things under control for us, Dad. I can't thank you both enough, and I want you to know we love you so.

"Hi, Mom, me too. I just told Dad of our love for the two of you. Lynn? Yeah, she's right here. I'll get her. Bye from me and hope to see you before snow and birth.

"Mom wants to speak with you, Babe. Here's the phone."

"Hi, Mom. I'm really fine and things could not be better for us.

"You did? Oh, that's wonderful, when will they move in?

"This coming week-end? If you don't mind, you and Dad keep the money in a fund. That would be great if you don't mind. Did you find the paperwork in the desk?

"Thank you so much for your help.

"I can't wait to go to town in a couple of days and get the mail. I'll set up a box at the local post office and let you know the address number. General delivery is fine for now and they know the Rolley family well here. Most of the town knows CJ and I are caring for Sheridan and will continue to do so. I'm so excited and bye Mom, love you lots. We'll be back to visit before Sheridan comes home. Love you, bye for now."

"Hey, isn't that super Lynn, Dad and Mom rented out our house. They were able to clean out all our personal stuff and papers. Dad made it a point to speak with our employers and bring them up to date. Our jobs will even be waiting for us if and when we return."

CJ was totally amazed and he knew how blessed he was with two parents that loved him and Lynn. They could not wait to see CJ and Lynn before Sheridan came home. After that would be winter and no great traveling. The roads would be tricky, Mr. Bowers could not be left alone, and the baby would be on its way.

Lynn ladled out the soup and placed two meat and cheese sandwiches on CJ's placemat. She then placed soup and a sandwich on her placemat, followed by two cups of hot chocolate, one for each of them.

The sky darkened while they ate, and soft rain sprinkled down. They both watched the droplets of water roll down the window panes and then disappear. Lynn told CJ how nice it was to talk to his parents, and it was especially good because it came with good news. Knowing the house was rented and that his mom and dad would handle collecting the rent and paying their mortgage was really fine.

"Mom also told me that I had received a letter postmarked from Romania. How wonderful. She said it was from my great aunt's daughter. I can't wait to tell her about the baby. She'll surely tell everyone she knows as soon as she gets the return letter I'll send her.

"Tomorrow I'm going to start going through the baby clothes and blankets that are in the foot locker.

I'll wash and dry them and see what we've got and what we need."

CJ said he would start on the baby furniture as soon as Lynn chose the pieces she wanted to use.

"If we wrap up loose ends this week, maybe we could go visit Mom and Dad for a couple of days."

"We probably could. I'm sure Donnie and his dad would stay up here or at least check in while we're gone and make sure the generator is working."

A few days later Lynn went to town to acquire a mail box and an accurate address for their mail. It was fortunate that Lynn had reached the bottom of the mountain trail before she met up with Donnie and his pick-up truck. He was just on his way up.

"Hi, Donnie," said Lynn, "I'm going to the post office to rent a mail box. CJ is up at Raven Hill just putting some finishing details on our reconditioned baby furniture. CJ will explain it all to you when you see him. Maybe I'll see you later, when I return from my list of chores for the day. I want to buy a few things before I return to Raven Hill. I've also got to get some more gas for the generator."

Donnie had some in the back of the pick-up truck also, which he made Lynn aware of.

"I think we might be able to come up with a better idea for electricity than the gas powered generator," he said, but all Lynn was able to think of was shopping and mail.

"Ok, whatever you guys agree on is fine with me. See you, Donnie, and thank you for all your help."

Donnie continued up the hill and Lynn continued out of town to the small strip mall they passed on their way to the hospital. Lynn pulled in the mall and found a parking space. She left the SUV and headed toward a store called The Baby Boutique. Once inside she oohed and aahed over the sweater sets, onesies, and the size of the clothes.

There it was, the item she came for. It was a newborn, long sleeved yellow shirt that had Daddy's Pride and Joy printed on it in all different colors. It was perfect. She also got a few little new born outfits and a new green sweater set with a giraffe on it. She paid her bill, grabbed the box they were packed in, and left the store feeling like a real mommy.

Next stop would be the post-office in Serpentine Gulch. She knew she would have to look closely or she would miss the alley way it was located on. It was off the beaten path and in the back porch of the postmaster's house. The porch was closed in and made weather worthy, but it was still a private house. Lynn entered the back of the house and called out hello. Soon an older gentleman walked out of the main section of his home to wait on her.

"Hi there," he said. "You must be CJ Rolley's kin, I mean wife."

"Yes, I'm his wife and my name is Lynn. I would like to secure a mail box for CJ and I."

"Well, as you can see there are no boxes, just slots in the wooden mail holder."

"Well, OK, how do I go about renting one?"

"You really don't need to rent one. We just sort your mail out by your last name and when you come in help yourself to yours if no one is here. Just put back what's not yours."

"That's it?" Lynn asked.

"That's it," she was told. "We're too small for formality. By the way everyone calls me Bud and my wife is Tess. Usually one of us is here if you need stamps or if you got a package going out."

"It was nice to meet you Bud."

"Oh, by the way, how is CJ's folks?"

"'They're fine. Now that we'll be living up on Raven Hill with Sheridan you will probably see them next spring."

"Living up on Raven Hill, huh. So they think old man Bowers will make it back home."

"He's doing very well, considering. He had pneumonia and then a stroke that left him very weak on his right side and he must learn to talk again, but he's improving daily and should be home by the end of October."

"Just in time to beat the snow. Raven Hill has always been a place with bad vibes since the time the Bowers buried Robert Jake. That would be Sheridan's great uncle's son, I guess.

"Oh, here, before I get off on a story let me give you some mail that came in today for you and CJ."

"Thanks, that's just what I was hoping for."

"I couldn't miss those foreign stamps on that one letter."

"Yes, it's from my great aunt's daughter. She's my only living relative, and I wish I could see her again. It's been many, many years since we last were together. Well, thank you for your time Bud, I must be headed back up the mountain. I've got things to do and the trail is time consuming to drive."

Lynn had gotten all she went for and was ready to go home. She found that she tired out more easily now and was thankful that CJ was larger built than she was. For the last week or so she borrowed his shirts for maternity blouses. The only clothes that seemed to fit her were elastic waist pants and skirts. She knew when they went back to visit Mom and Dad next week, she and Mom would go shopping for some clothes for her and maybe they would check out baby clothes too. She could not wait to see CJ's folks, but right now reading her letter from Romania was top priority.

She crested the top of the mountain and there were CJ and Donnie wandering from shed to shed and enjoying themselves. Lynn blew the horn and waved as she drove down to the cabin. On the table were empty coffee cups and cupcake wrappers. The guys had been there, too. She didn't care, she wanted to read her mail from her great aunt's daughter, Gina. In Romania everyone is family. As long as they get along and help each other, they're family.

Lynn was not sure of her true relationship to Gina, but daughter of her great aunt was fine with her. The letter started with talk of the great distance between them, and how much Gina missed Lynn. The fact that she was no spring chicken worried her that she may never see Lynn again. She had a lot of questions about her and CJ: were they still living in the same area near CJ's folks, would there ever be news of their starting a family? She wanted to be there when that happened.

Doctors and hospitals would be out of the question. Gina had been a mid-wife for years and more than capable of bringing a child into this world. After all, she did mid-wifing for every member of their community in Romania. Time was going so fast and how Gina's heart longed for Lynn. She finished the letter, "Please write and up date me on your life in the USA. With much love and longing, Gina."

Lynn immediately started a letter back to her, telling her all about Raven Hill and Sheridan Bowers and how CJ was going to inherit the mountain when Sheridan passed. She also told Gina how Mr. Bowers' health was and that she would be caring for him up on Raven Hill.

She rambled on about all kinds of things and childhood memories and then told Gina about her pregnancy and that she would deliver in first week of February. She and CJ would have to decide how all this was going to play out with him and the birth of the new baby, but she was going to look into the possibility of finding a mountain mid-wife for her delivery. She was healthy and she had been to a doctor who would be seeing her again to confirm the health of her baby and her. "Please write very soon Gina, I miss family."

Lynn was so glad to hear from Gina and be able to write back so soon, but she was also feeling a little blue. She missed her childhood days and her mom and dad and the visits to and from Romania to see relatives and friends. Now it was just a memory, and a blurred one at that.

All of a sudden she remembered Donnie was still outside with CJ. She grabbed her letter to Gina and went to the desk to affix some postage to it, then out the door to find Donnie. Lynn left the porch and made a right turn up the little beaten path to the sheds. Sure enough there were Donnie and CJ checking over old tools and reminiscing about their younger days.

"Hi Donnie, would you do me a big favor?"

"Well, I'll try to, Lynn."

"Would you please mail this letter for me? I'm sure there's more than enough postage on it, but here is another dollar, just in case."

You hold on to the dollar and if it needs more stamps, I'll let you know all about it next time I see you."

"If you're sure. Thanks again, Donnie. I don't think we could make it without you and your father's help."

Donnie smiled and then went back to talking to CJ about tools and the past.

Lynn walked over to where the baby furniture was drying in the breeze. CJ had cleaned off all the years of dirt and dust from storage, then he had revarnished each piece .The furniture glistened in the sunlight and it took on the look of newly made and lovely carved heirloom pieces. Mrs. Bowers must have felt so loved and thrilled to have these items, to know they were made by her family with such love.

A baby bed was made by the prior generation, but Pa Bowers made the high chair and the wooden walker. Back in those days the walker was a permanent seat on a flat base with no wheels for movement. They did not want baby to get to the lanterns or the fireplace or get underfoot in the kitchen. The cabin could be a dangerous place for a little one.

Toys were given to them and there was a tray for snacks .With families usually being large, there was always someone to entertain baby. Lynn really liked the idea of using the Bowers heirloom furniture for their child.

While Lynn was locked in her daydreams, Donnie and CJ had finished their conversation and small talk. Donnie had said his good byes to CJ and wandered over to where Lynn was admiring the furniture.

"That's real good furniture," said Donnie. Them Bowers men can really work wood. You would never find such beautiful detail in the wood as these pieces have, no way. This furniture was made for kin, and it was special worked with much love and prayers. I think it is real proper that you want CJ and your little one to share in the history and love of this furniture. After all, only kin would be allowed to use it.

"I'm figuring that Sheridan would have normally destroyed these items. He must have been thinking real deep about CJ to save them and turn them over to you and him for your baby. Yeah, Sheridan surely accepted CJ as one of his, or you would have never seen this baby furniture in one piece."

"Well, I guess that's good then," said Lynn, looking at Donnie.

"Yes ma'am, I think so, and it's real good to hear that there will be some new life up here on the mountain. I can't wait to tell my Pa about it."

"Please come back real soon, Donnie, and bring your Pa with you."

"He thinks of you two as family, too."

Donnie looked at Lynn then back to CJ. He then opened the door of his truck, which was close by, and got in. The pick-up started. Donnie waved and headed down the hill to deposit Lynn's letter into a mail receptacle outside the post office, then he was going home to do some chores and feed the dogs.

Lynn and CJ watched as his truck dropped out of sight. CJ checked to see if the varnish on the baby furniture was dry. It was, so they carried the pieces back to the cabin and placed them in the baby's room for safe keeping.

Lynn put another piece of wood into the stove to heat water for hot drinks. It was late afternoon and it was chilly outside. Two cups of cocoa were placed on the table and the two of them sat down to talk and relax. They decided to go visit CJ's folks the next day. He had discussed their trip back home with Donnie. He and his Pa would be watching over Raven Hill while they were gone. Lynn was thrilled to be going to see CJ's parents again. Since her parents had passed away years ago, she had grown fond and loving of her in-laws and she thought of them as her parents, too.

CJ called his folks as Lynn removed the empty cups from the table. She decided to start packing for their two day stay at the in-laws. That would give CJ time to update them on the baby furniture and let them know they got the mail from home and that the out of country letter was from Lynn's great aunt's daughter Gina.

When Lynn passed by the baby room she smiled with anticipation of the coming little one, and how she and CJ would hold and play with this little bundle. She was already planning its life and it was not here yet. On the way to her bedroom she would have to pass by the other bedroom, the one for Sheridan, with his personal needs in it; his clothes, shoes, commode, and his favorite old books, that he read and reread for pleasure.

Lynn was not smiling at the sights in that room. She was almost annoyed and disgusted by the fact he would be coming home and they would have to tend to his needs. She got a grip on her thoughts of anger, and felt ashamed of how every once in a while it was like she was not herself. She liked Sheridan and she was thankful to him and for him. Why did these selfish and mean flashes enter her mind? She figured it was because she was pregnant and her hormones were running rampant, and it was not the most ideal situation, although it was far from unbearable.

She continued to her bedroom to pack clothes for her and CJ's trip tomorrow. CJ was busy talking to his Mom, not his Dad. Mom was planning a quick baby shower for Lynn. Between CJ and his Mom, things had been worked out pretty well. It would be a wonderful surprise for Lynn to have her friends and CJ's folks throw this party. Mom knew there would be many things Lynn would need for the little one. It was going to be great fun.

With the need for baby furniture supplied, Mom was really having a hard time trying to figure out what to get for Lynn and CJ. It only took her a few seconds and she was able to think of something wonderful. It was so good that she did not even want to tell CJ. It would be a surprise for him, too.

Chapter 12

*T*he visit back home for the next two days was great. The first day Lynn and Mom went shopping for maternity clothes and a couple of new outfits for the little one Lynn was carrying. Lynn really wanted to shop longer, but her legs and feet ached and she could see Mom was tired, too.

That night the party was a hit. Girl friends came from near and far to celebrate the pregnancy. Guys showed up to congratulate CJ and to talk about the new adventure living up on Raven Hill. The night was a great success, and Lynn and CJ got tons of baby goodies. They truly needed nothing else. All the women at the party helped to clean up when it was over. Mom promised to let them all know when the baby was born and if it was a he or a she.

All went home and the four Rolleys went to bed. They were all exhausted and at peace. The four of them slept in, not waking until after 10:30. None of them normally slept that late, but it had been a long day yesterday. Long and good. The next day was quiet and privately enjoyed by the four of them. Mom and Lynn washed and folded baby clothes so they would be ready for the birth. Dad and CJ talked over the house rental and finalized how and when to pay bills concerning the mortgage and taxes.

The four of them went out for supper on the last night of the visit. They just talked and laughed about the past and the future. During a moment of quiet, Mom turned to CJ and Lynn and said that she and Dad had started a savings account for their grandchild. They also had another gift for the two of them, but thought it best to inform them before they set it in action. CJ and Lynn looked at each other then back to Mom and Dad with a look of puzzlement on their faces. What did Mom mean by putting in into action?

"Well, we know that the two of you have been concerned about Sheridan's needs and the pregnancy, as well as the birth of the baby. How were you going to deal with all of it? It was more than the two of you could easily handle. I had a long talk with Lynn's great aunt's daughter a few days ago. She would be more than willing to come visit and stay with the three of you up on Raven Hill from early January to the first of March. This way she could help with Sheridan's needs, which would give Lynn time to relax and take some of the worry off your mind, CJ.

"She would also be there for the birth of the baby. She is a fully certified mid-wife and more than capable of delivery. There is nothing she has not seen and done when it comes to obstetrics. It will mean sharing your place with another person for awhile, and it would also mean leaning on Sheridan's good nature, too. But we think it might be good for all and Lynn would be able to enjoy Gina's company. Gina is on hold and waiting for a phone call from Dad and I. We will pay for everything. It's our gift to the two of you and our grandchild."

Lynn hugged Mom and cried. CJ was relieved of many of his fears over the birth of the baby and the worry over the pressure that would be on Lynn with Sheridan and a new born. Mom looked at the reaction from CJ and Lynn and said, "When we get home we will call Gina and confirm a date."

Dad asked CJ about getting her up the mountain.

"If you can get her to Serpentine Gulch, I can get her up the mountain, even if I've got to borrow a horse and sleigh."

They all laughed and slowly wrapped up their night out and headed back to Mom and Dad's place to make that phone call to Romania. Once home, Mom placed a call to Gina. Between the five of them interjecting ideas and thoughts the plan was secured. Gina would receive money for expenses to travel from Romania to Serpentine Gulch, USA, where CJ would meet her at the closest airport and escort her up to Raven Hill for a nice long visit. Lynn got to speak with Gina and everything was going to be perfect for Sheridan, CJ, Lynn, Gina, and the little one to come.

The trip back to Raven Hill was light and welcomed. All the worries that were unsettled two days prior were gone and the sun was brighter than ever. Everything was turning out to be great. Everyone's needs would be covered and Lynn and Gina would have time to bond again and talk over old times. Gina would be able to up-date Lynn on things and people. Lynn would be able to tell Gina about the passing of her parents and how CJ's parents were such a blessing to her.

Donnie was out by his pick-up truck as Lynn and CJ drove past his cabin on their way to Raven Hill. CJ blew the horn and he and Lynn waved to Donnie, who returned the greeting. Up the mountain and over the crest of the hill went the SUV. There stood Raven Hill with open arms waiting to comfort and embrace them back home. That's the way Lynn always thought of it. CJ was still watching for the birds to return; he just could not totally accept things could be so perfect for them. Lynn had called him pessimistic and negative at times, but his Dad said he was a true realist, not a person to easily given to false hopes and beliefs. CJ thought it best to stay on his guard, without letting on anything bothered him.

Sheridan was doing very well with his therapy sessions although he was not yet able to walk well. He was able to take a few steps and pivot on his feet with the help of a walker. He had not regained his ability to speak well either, but he was doing much better, and if one was to listen carefully to him he could make his words understood. It was a sure thing Sheridan would be coming home at the end of October, actually on Halloween. Between CJ, Lynn, Donnie, and Donnie's Pa everything was ready for Sheridan Bowers to return to Raven Hill.

The month of September was cold and windy up on the hill, but still the three guys were able to install a water powered generator from the mountain springs that never froze over. That was a great savings on gas and one less thing for CJ to worry about. They were also able to find Lynn a washing machine for the back porch which they closed in. She would still be hanging clothes outside if the snow was not too bad. The wind blew constantly up on Raven Hill so the clothes would dry outside or in if need be.

Lynn again was thrilled. She was getting quite a belly on her and hand washing clothes for even just her and CJ was getting to be a real chore. Soon she would also have Sheridan's clothes and a few months after that there would be the little one's clothes as well.

She had let her hair transition from the last dye job and it was finally her natural color, dark ebony brown. She was more beautiful than ever in CJ's eyes. The pregnancy and the fresh mountain air had really put the bloom in her natural beauty.

Chapter 13

The day finally came when Sheridan was to be air lifted home. He was uneasy about the flight but he was ready to go home. He was much stronger and much healthier. He was looking and feeling unstoppable. CJ was on the phone with Dr. Miles as they prepared Sheridan for lift off. The doctor would be traveling with him back to Raven Hill for Sheridan's comfort and for any last minute questions Lynn or CJ may have concerning his care.

"Well, we're loaded on CJ, can you hear me over the props?"

"Yes, but barely, Doctor."

"All is well. We're lifting up and the pilot is headed toward Raven Hill."

"Good, good," said CJ. "Is Sheridan OK?"

There was silence, nothing, no response.

"Oh, my word, CJ! The birds are right behind us and gaining. The damn things are following us, if that's possible. If they get any closer… The pilot is looking for a place to land. Wait, wait, CJ, they're backing off, they're still following, but not as close. We should be there in about 10 minutes."

CJ looked at Lynn and said, "Lynn, please go to the house and make coffee for us all."

"What are you talking about? I want to be here when Sheridan lands."

"Please go to the house, before they get here. I'll explain later. Go now, Lynn. If you love me, go now."

Lynn was angry and hurt by CJ's demand. She could hear the helicopter cutting through the air as it headed for the clearing. Then she saw the birds trailing behind Sheridan.

"Oh my Lord, what is going on," she said under her breath.

The helicopter landed and the birds dive bombed the aircraft as well as CJ, Donnie, and his father. They were pecking and scratching the three men outside the aircraft. All three of the men were running toward the sheds for protection from the assault upon them. Everyone was in disbelief. The birds were battering themselves against the dome of the helicopter. Many ravens lay dead from the attack and many others were wounded and dying.

Lynn raced toward the shed were CJ, Donnie, and his Dad were. The birds were literally trying to peck and claw the shed apart to get to them. Sheridan, Dr. Miles, and the pilot were safe but unable to fly away from the scene. All they could do was watch in disbelief.

Lynn screamed at the birds on the shed. She grabbed a piece of a broken tree limb and swung it at the birds all the while screaming, "No! Go away! No!"

CJ heard her screams and bolted out of the shed. He wrapped his arms around her and tucked her head into his chest to protect her from any attacks. The birds stopped immediately and froze in position, until one of them headed toward the oak tree in the cemetery to roost on its branch. Half of them flew to the oak tree and sat quietly watching the humans and the aircraft. The other half flew down the side of the mountain and disappeared. CJ took Lynn, Donnie, and Donnie's father to the cabin.

Emotions were running high with fear, disbelief, and total confusion. Safely inside, CJ called Dr. Miles in the helicopter. He answered his phone with, "What was that, CJ?"

Sheridan was babbling and CJ could hear him, but not understand what he was saying.

"Is Sheridan OK?" asked CJ.

"He's like the rest of us, in shock," answered Miles. The pilot is going to return to the hospital with Sheridan. It's not safe with those birds attacking."

Sheridan was clearly saying no to that statement. Everyone in the cabin could understand his wanting to stay home, he'd been gone so long.

"No, don't go, please Dr. Miles. Let us fire off a few rounds at the birds that are left. I'm sure they will leave. Please don't take Sheridan back to the hospital if he's OK and I would really appreciate if you would check out Lynn before you leave."

"Go ahead and shoot, we'll see what happens."

CJ and the two men each took a gun off the mantel. CJ handed them shells. With guns loaded out the door they went. Lynn was riveted to the window watching. The men aimed and shot. Ravens fell all over, only a few were able to fly away. All was silent. No birds were to be seen, except for the ones that committed suicide and ones that caught lead. After waiting several minutes the men walked up to the landing. The helicopter was covered with blood and feathers.

Donnie and CJ kicked dead birds out of the way of the door. Dr. Miles opened the door and between the three men and Dr. Miles they were able to get Sheridan into the cabin. The pilot stayed behind to clean some of the mess off the aircraft and ready it for the return flight.

Dr. Miles helped to get Sheridan comfortable and he then checked on his vitals. All was good, that old man was tough. He then went with Lynn into her room to check on her health and to take her vitals as well. He thought Lynn and Sheridan would both be fine.

He patched up CJ, Donnie, and his Dad before he headed toward the helicopter. The birds had pecked holes in the men. Donnie walked the doctor to the landing and saw him off. Still no birds appeared.

Donnie and his Dad decided to spend the night, CJ and Lynn could use the support. Sheridan was so glad to be home he napped. CJ figured Sheridan had probably seen worse things happen than this. He knew Sheridan had gone up against bears, bucks and snakes in his life time that had to have been a lot worse.

Later that evening, after they all had a chance to draw their own conclusions about the events of the day, Lynn rustled up a light supper for everyone. They sat Sheridan up in his favorite chair which they had moved into his room. Donnie and his Pa carried the small kitchen table into Sheridan's room so they could all dine together. The closeness they shared in Sheridan's bedroom gave them a feeling of safety in numbers.

Lynn cleaned up the supper dishes and the men helped Sheridan get more comfortable and ready for bed. It was obvious that he was exhausted, but happy to be in his own surroundings. The men got him into bed and made sure his needs were met, such as a glass of water on his bedside table, his spelling board, his Bible, and his bell that would summons Lynn and CJ if he needed help.

Donnie and his Pa bid Sheridan good night and went to the sitting room to wait for CJ. CJ looked around and felt secure that he had done all he could for Pa Bowers.

"Well, good night, Pa. I'm sorry your coming home turned into such an unexplainable mess. But I'm glad you're here and I hope you're not too uncomfortable in your own home with all of us sharing your domain."

Pa looked at CJ and smiled as he shook his head no. CJ went to go out the door when he heard Pa try to speak to him. He turned back and Pa had his spelling board in his lap. CJ went closer to the bed and Pa spelled "curse" over and over. Then he spelled "ravens". CJ cringed at the thought of a curse, but the intensity in Pa's eyes really made his skin crawl.

CJ looked at Pa and said, "I'm concerned, too, but I don't know at this point what to do. Sometimes for strange reasons animals and birds act weird. It would not be the first time something like this has happened, I'm sure. As far as curses go, Pa, I love and respect you, but I have a hard time blaming this on some curse that happened years and years ago. If that was the case why hasn't something happened before this?"

Pa spelled out, "Everything in its own time."

"Get some sleep, Pa, if you need anything ring your bell. I'll leave the door cracked open so we can hear you ring."

Sheridan waved in agreement to CJ and then snuggled down into his bed for rest. Lynn had made up beds on the two sofas in the sitting room for the two guests. They all decided to get a good night's sleep and rethink what had occurred in the morning.

Within a few minutes everyone was in their beds except for CJ. He wanted to check in on Sheridan before retiring. He tip-toed into Sheridan's room and checked to see if he was breathing easily. He was, so CJ sat down in the chair at the end of Sheridan's bed and watched him sleep as well as survey the cemetery and its absence of life, human or fowl. The only noise CJ was aware of was the sound of each person's sleep music.

Pa, who was a loud snorer when CJ was a child, would make what Ma Bowers called "sleep music" all night. When the kids would tease or complain about their father's loud snoring, Ma Bowers would say, "Thank God for that sleep music, it means your father is still with us and resting well."

CJ quietly exited the bedroom and headed up the hall to his and Lynn's bedroom. Lynn, too, was sound asleep and making her soft music. She was filling out well rounded and becoming heavy with child. The baby was now moving inside her, and CJ was thrilled to see this happen. He was hoping that living up on Raven Hill would be a wonderful life for all of them. Now he was becoming more uneasy with the return of the birds, and watching Lynn running after the birds with a stick as her baby pounced inside of her. What was happening and why now? He curled around Lynn and the baby and drifted off to sleep making his own music.

They all slept long and sound. CJ awoke to the sound of Sheridan ringing his bell for assistance. Before CJ could get his pants on, the ringing ceased. He finished putting his jeans on and headed down the hall. Donnie's dad had helped Sheridan and was now coming out of the bedroom .Donnie had started the stove and made coffee for all of them. CJ was glad that Donnie and his dad were comfortable enough to make themselves at home. Donnie thought CJ should walk out on the back porch and take a look at the cemetery. He could feel the blood drain from his face at Donnie's insistence.

He opened the back door and stepped out onto the porch. With eyes locked fully open he surveyed the cemetery. They were back, and they blackened the old oak tree that held them. They seemed quiet and unthreatening, but their presence was unnerving. While the men stood out on the porch observing the ravens in the tree, Lynn awoke and dressed for the day, unaware of the feathered stalkers. She started down the hall and headed to the back door to take her early morning walk to the privy.

"What's going on out here guys, please let me squeeze by."

"Where are you going, Lynn?" asked CJ.

"Well, I'm 6 months pregnant and have been sleeping for the last 8 hours. I'm on a mission to the outhouse."

"Wait, let me get my shoes on and I'll walk with you."

"Why, CJ?"

Donnie nodded in the direction of the cemetery and Lynn froze at the sight of the ravens perched all over the tree. As Lynn observed the birds CJ slipped on his boots and readied himself for the morning jaunt. Donnie handed CJ a gun and stood sentry on the back porch until their return. The birds never let on they saw them. The winged creatures seemed preoccupied, grooming themselves in the crisp autumn air.

Back inside Lynn started breakfast while the men helped Sheridan take care of his morning needs and get dressed for the day. With help Sheridan was able to slowly make it down the hall and into the sitting room by the fireplace. This was where he was most comfortable and his chair was perfectly placed, offering him views of the property and its sheds, driveway, and the cemetery. The men helped him to his chair and Lynn brought him a hot cup of coffee to sip while the bacon fried.

He sat down and acknowledged with a nod and a smile the coffee Lynn placed on the table in front of him. The men sat down on the sofas without saying a word. Sheridan surveyed the cleanliness of the room and how clean and sweet the cabin smelled. He waved his hand at Lynn and she understood he approved of her ability to clean. He then started to look out the windows, which was affirming to him he was home again. He saw the driveway and the sheds and how the property had been tidied up. He also noticed the stack of firewood had grown since he was hospitalized.

Then he noticed the visitors in the cemetery. He first looked at the mantel for the guns, then at the men who had them sitting next to the back door ready for action. He picked up his spelling board and started to spell. "Must find out reason. Must be on guard."

Lynn was placing a stack of pancakes and bacon on the kitchen table for the guys to enjoy. She had already made a special plate for Sheridan that was cut and ready to eat. She put a small glass of syrup on the tray and placed it in front of him, so he could easily partake. The rest of them went to the table and ate after praying thanks for the food. Sheridan was saying his own prayers under his breathe as he ate and watched the birds groom themselves.

With everyone full from breakfast, and all giving a little help for cleanup, the two men announced that they should be on their way home. The dogs were probably pretty hungry, since they missed yesterday's meal and the both of them had chores to do and errands to run.

"Is there anything else we can do before we mosey on down the mountain?" asked Donnie of CJ and Lynn.

"No," said CJ, "we are truly thankful again for your help, and for staying the night in case we had a problem."

Sheridan looked as peaceful as could be under the circumstances. He was not an alarmist under any conditions, just quiet, analytical, and ready for what action might be needed. Donnie's Pa went into the sitting room to say good-byes from him and his son, as well as thanks for allowing them to spend the night. It was the proper thing to do, after all it was still Sheridan's home. Sheridan reached out for Donnie's father's hand and he grasped it and smiled at his old friend. Love and integrity was the bond that made them friends, even before the kids were born.

Donnie told CJ, "Considering my pick-up is out by the far shed, our going out there will be a test for the birds."

He said that his Pa had went outside before anyone was up and the birds never bothered him at all. "Matter a fact he didn't see or hear them as he walked up to the water generator to check it out. Now I grant you he wasn't under them, but I'm sure they could see him trailing up the slope to the clearing. He said he took time to look over the battle area from yesterday and still no problems occurred."

The two of them stood in the kitchen area and both admitted they had no idea what happened and neither had heard or seen anything like this before. CJ grabbed his gun and walked the two men outside to their truck cautiously. The ravens seem to be oblivious to their presence. They got into the truck and assured CJ that they would be back up the following day with their dogs. Maybe they would chase away the birds.

"Sounds like a good idea to me," said CJ.

The truck started up and slowly moved to the top of the mountain road -- still no action from the birds. CJ grabbed some more wood for the stove and headed back to the cabin for another cup of coffee and a talk with Pa Bowers. After placing the wood in the wood box by the stove, he picked up the coffee pot and a cup and headed to the sitting room to be with Sheridan. Lynn was in the bedrooms making beds and cleaning up, so this was a good time for the two of them to talk.

CJ reached over to Sheridan's cup and filled it half way. Then he poured the rest into his cup and sat down to talk. Placing the coffee pot on the fireplace hearth, he picked up his cup and they both looked out the window to watch the birds.

"Pa, why is this happening and has it happened in the past that you know of?"

"It is the curse of Robert Jake."

"Has it happened before?"

"A few ravens were always in the old oak tree but never caused harm. It's a sign of more to come son. Watch and be alert. Don't be afraid, be aware and ready." The old man laid down his spelling board and picked up his coffee.

CJ picked up the coffee pot and his cup and headed to the kitchen. Lynn was coming down the hall with Sheridan's book he was reading. She placed it within his reach and returned to the kitchen to drink the rest of her tea. Lynn asked CJ if he thought she could use the oven in the kitchen stove.

"Sure, I'll stoke up the stove and explain how it works and then enjoy yourself."

Lynn was going to bake a couple of apple pies. The apples she'd purchased a while back were getting brown spots, so it was time for pie and they all liked apple pie especially in the autumn .She understood the workings of the oven after a quick run through. CJ had purchased a couple of fire extinguishers, one for the stove and one for the fireplace, so everything was ready and safe for pie making.

Sheridan listened to the kitchen talk with his eyes closed. His thoughts would drift from subject to subject until he found a thought that would carry him off to sleep. He was on that excursion as he heard the talk about apple pie, his favorite dessert.

Lynn busied herself with peeling apples and making crust while CJ took this opportunity to slip outside and really test the ravens. He knew they wanted him yesterday, along with Donnie and his father. Today he would make a brave stand and continue his outside work as if they were not there and nothing ever happened yesterday, but still his shotgun would be near.

He worked outside for hours and even forgot about the stalkers in the tree. Every once in awhile he would catch the smell of apple pie in the air. Finally he heard Lynn call to him from the front porch. CJ grabbed his gun and headed to the cabin to assist her. Once inside he learned that Sheridan had a nature call he needed to answer. CJ helped him to his bedroom and the commode.

The whole house smelled like apple pie and the kitchen was warm from the stove. While Sheridan was indisposed, CJ started a small fire in the fireplace to take the chill out of the sitting room. This would make Sheridan more comfortable since his body was still healing and his thermostat would not always stoke up the heat for his own warmth. CJ returned Pa Bowers to his loved spot in the sitting room and Lynn brought him some hot soup, a ham sandwich, more of his beloved coffee, and a slice of homemade apple pie. Pa Bowers was looking at a feast and he was grateful.

After lunch CJ helped Pa back to his room for therapy followed by a nice nap. The first day home and things were working out alright, and if this was how it would be, it was a going to be a piece of pie. The rest of the day was uneventful and quiet. The three tenants of Raven Hill simply enjoyed themselves with simple chores.

That night after supper CJ helped Sheridan into bed and checked on him later to be sure he was comfortably sleeping.

Lynn and CJ sat by the fireplace and reminisced their lives from the time they met until now. They could not believe the chain of events that brought them together. Their backgrounds were totally different. He was English and Welsh. Lynn was not sure what her heritage was, she thought probably she was English also -- after all, her maiden name was Mason.

Lynn was getting tired and so was CJ so they thought it best to head for bed. Lynn decided to mark off the days on the calendar before she turned in for the night. CJ was already in bed watching Lynn survey and cross off the days until Gina would be there and then when the baby would be due.

Suddenly Lynn looked at CJ and said, "Tomorrow I'm supposed to be at the hospital for my baby check-up. With all that happened I forgot."

"Don't worry, it will be fine. Donnie and his dad are coming up early with the dogs. I'm sure they will hold down the fort until we get back. Maybe it will be really good for Sheridan to be able to pass some time with his old friend."

OK, that's settled then. Tomorrow we can go for the baby appointment and Donnie and his dad will stay with Sheridan."

All slept through the night with no disturbances. Morning found Lynn making some French toast for breakfast and CJ was helping Pa to get comfortable for the day in the sitting room. The birds were status quo in the oak tree and the smell of breakfast was wafting through the cabin. The three of them enjoyed their meal, and Pa even tried to say grace. Although it was really hard to understand what he was saying, it was said with great feeling and reverence.

CJ explained to Sheridan that Donnie and his pa would be coming up this morning to chase the birds with the coon hounds they had. He also told Pa that Lynn had a doctor's visit today at the hospital. They were going to see the baby she was carrying with the help of a machine. CJ told Pa that they should not be too long in the city, and that Donnie would see to his needs and lunch.

Pa nodded with approval. He used his spelling board to ask if he could also see the picture of the baby when they got back. Lynn piped up and said he surely could, after all, he was going to be the Great-pa. Sheridan still was not sure how he felt about that title, but he thought he was being given a respectful opportunity to be part of this little one's life and that was good.

Lynn and CJ cleaned up the dishes and the kitchen. While Lynn made beds and tidied up the bedrooms, CJ made sure the fireplace was going and the cabin would be warm and cozy for Sheridan, who was actually able to say "Donnie" as he motioned to the window.

There was Donnie's pick-up coming over the crest of the hill. He pulled the truck over by the last shed where he always parked and he and his pa got out and started toward the house. CJ met them half way across the yard. There they exchanged greetings and CJ asked if they could stay with Sheridan until they returned from the doctor's. With everyone able to fulfill a need, they ambled toward the cabin with the two Pas waving to each other.

The coon hounds where in the back of the truck, and they wanted out. They had been up here before and they loved the woods and the open space, and Pa Bowers loved to hear them bark and howl as they covered the mountain top. Lynn and CJ got ready to make the trip to town.

"Now please help yourself to whatever you men want. We'll be bringing back some more groceries, so enjoy. Oh, by the way, there is some homemade apple pie under the towel. I think Sheridan would like that and some fresh coffee with his lunch. Where are the dogs?" asked Lynn.

Donnie's Pa said they were in the cage in the back of the truck. "They'll be let out after you're out of sight. They might try to follow you, so we'll wait till you're gone."

CJ and Lynn said their good byes and thank yous and headed down the mountain toward the city hospital. Donnie let the dogs loose and they took off running and barking through the woods. Sheridan watched out the window and laughed at the joy the dogs showed.

They got to the hospital with time to spare for Lynn's appointment. The news vans were gone, so were the spectators, all because the birds were nowhere to be seen, neither was their mess. It was like they were never there at all. No one even spoke about the curtain of birds being gone.

CJ waited in the lounge for Lynn to be examined by Dr. Adams. When it was over, he was asked to meet his wife and the doctor in the x-ray department. The doctor stood by while Lynn had her sonogram and she explained to the expectant parents what they were seeing. CJ and Lynn both chose not to know the sex of the baby, but they did want to know that he or she was well. There the child was on the screen. All parts in the right place and bouncing around happy and contented.

Dr. Adams said things looked real good, and she had no concerns at all. Mom and Baby were thriving. She gave Lynn another appointment for the following month, but there was a possibility that Lynn may not make it with winter coming. Dr. Adams told her to call if there was a problem, for there is always air lift. They left the hospital and headed off to get some lunch and do a little grocery shopping.

After doing all the day required of them, the two parents-to-be headed back home to Raven Hill. The mountain climb was always beautiful and quiet. It was like entering another time. No communities, rapid transportation, or noise, just nature.

As they drove into the yard, the oak was still holding the birds, who were still just grooming themselves. CJ said he did not think they would be there much longer because winter and its snow would be coming. Birds usually find warm places to nest down in and keep warm till spring.

Inside the cabin sat the three men not saying much and not looking happy at all. They just turned and looked at the two as they walked in. CJ placed two large bags of groceries on the table and turned to the door to go fetch two more. Donnie wiped his eyes and followed CJ out the door. Lynn walked over to Sheridan and handed him a sonogram picture of the baby she was carrying. Sheridan looked preoccupied, but he reached out and accepted the snapshot willingly.

"Is there something wrong?" she asked Donnie's Pa.

He looked at Sheridan and answered that they all had a lunch and that the apple pie was real good. He then got up and nodded at Sheridan as he went out the door.

Sheridan watched Lynn put the groceries away. She poured a glass of orange juice and placed it in front of Sheridan. He picked it up and sipped it as he watched out the window. The three guys outside were standing by the back of the truck. Donnie was really heartbroken and it was noticeable to Sheridan.

"CJ," Donnie said, "it was unbelievable, how those birds attacked the two dogs without reason. The dogs never did bother with them at all. They didn't even bark at them in the tree. The next thing we know, we were just finishing up our lunch when we heard the dogs barking and growling and whimpering something awful. Pa and I thought for sure they rousted out a bear that was standing its ground against them. I grabbed a shotgun and shells and headed out the door. Pa stayed with Sheridan and the two of them watched from the windows. The dogs were up on the landing and the ravens were in full attack. There were as many birds as there were the day the helicopter landed with Sheridan.

"I shot and killed a mess of them, but not in time to stop the birds from forcing the dogs to the side of the mountain and pushing them off. The poor things were half dead at that point anyhow, but the birds acted like they were revenging the day we killed a bunch of them. They showed no mercy. Once the dogs went over the side, half went back to the oak tree and half took off down the mountain again. They never bothered me, they just watched as I roped and was able to retrieve my hunters. One lay dead and the other died shortly after I got him back up off the ledge.

"There is blood, dog hair, feathers, and dead birds galore up there. I'm just sick about losing those dogs. Are you sure you want to continue to live up here with those birds, CJ? It's like they're going crazy."

The two mountain men decided they would be going home to bury their dogs. They reassured CJ that Sheridan was fine, probably just very tired. He ate well but he did not have a nap. CJ was so sorry about the dogs, he too loved those blue tick hounds. They were such big strong dogs that it was hard to conceive that birds could kill them. These mountain ravens were not to be believed or understood.

The old truck went over the mountain and CJ stood looking at the oak tree and the ravens. He felt so bad this had occurred, especially when the guys were helping him and Lynn. CJ headed toward the house with a shotgun in his right hand and some logs in his left arm to feed the fireplace with.

Lynn was just finishing up with Sheridan's exercises as CJ walked though the front door. She rushed to take the wood from his arm and CJ hung the gun back up on the mantle. He and Sheridan exchanged glances. Lynn announced that supper would be ready in two minutes. She set the tables and Sheridan's tray. It was fried chicken and all the trimmings. They ate quietly and then settled down with hot drinks to talk.

Lynn asked Sheridan what he thought of the baby picture. He picked it up and looked at it again. He then passed it to CJ and picked up his spelling board. He spelled, "So small. Is it a boy or a girl?"

Lynn said they did not want to know. It was going to be a surprise. CJ and Sheridan could not help to exchange solemn looks at each other as they sat there. Lynn could feel something was not right.

"How was your day while we were gone, Sheridan?" she asked.

CJ looked at Sheridan and spoke. "Lynn, something happened today that was unbelievable and sad.

"What was it, CJ?" she asked.

"Donnie let his dogs run free after we left as he said he was going to do. Things I guess were fine until after lunch. The dogs were up on the landing and for some reason the ravens attacked and killed them both."

"That's impossible, CJ. It must have been a bear or buck. Ravens couldn't kill those big dogs. They're hunting dogs, they kill coons and raccoons are mean warriors."

"I know, I thought the same thing and so did Donnie. He got to the landing in time to help the dogs by shooting some of the birds, but he also witnessed the dogs demise."

"Why is this happening, CJ?"

"Pa thinks it's a curse from generations ago."

Lynn looked at Sheridan and he nodded yes. Lynn did not believe in curses.

"Maybe we can call some wildlife person to help us rid ourselves of these birds. Winter is just around the corner and I think they will all leave then. They don't seem to bother people anymore. Now it's dogs."

The rest of the evening was spent with the two of them talking about how and why the dogs might have triggered the attack on them. Sheridan listened with eyes closed and only once in awhile he would tap out words on his spelling board. CJ was prompted by Sheridan to help him get to bed for the night. He was bushed and ever since he had come home there had been little peace. The three of them tucked in for the night with hopes that tomorrow would be better.

Chapter 14

*T*he next couple of months were very uneventful up on Raven Hill. Lynn had mastered her chores and although she and Sheridan would butt heads occasionally, nothing would come from it. The next day things would be forgotten. CJ continued to work around the yard making sure things were ready for the big snow which would eventually fall. They had woken several mornings to heavy frost and they had even had slight snow overnight and in the afternoons. None of those downfalls had amounted to much.

As far as Donnie and his Pa, they still came up to Raven Hill to visit. They would still give of their time to sit with Sheridan while CJ and Lynn went to her doctor's appointments and Lynn invited them up for a Thanksgiving meal that had all the trimmings. Rarely was their talk about the ravens, but there they were, sitting in the tree night and day. The snow would collect on their feathers and they looked like they were shivering, but they would not leave the cemetery. Everyone was aware of their presence, but since they caused no harm, at times they were overlooked.

Lynn continued to grow larger and more tired as time went on. Her health and the baby's health were perfect. Her doctor was contented with all facets of Lynn's pregnancy. She and CJ were getting a little impatient waiting for the arrival. It was now two weeks before Christmas and CJ's folks called to say hi and see how all were doing. He told them things were good and Sheridan was stronger and able to sound out more words now. He was doing so well that he seldom had to use his spelling board, he only had to talk slowly to be understood. Now he was able to walk from room to room with his walker, carefully and slowly, but still he was gaining ground. Doing his therapy exercises with him three times a day truly paid off for all of them.

Lynn spoke with her mother-in-law about her thoughts on the baby, and how her doctor was comfortable with the pregnancy. Mom informed Lynn that she had been in touch with Gina several times, that Gina had received the money and that she had purchased her ticket, so everything was looking good.

They both were amazed how light the snow had been so far. This would be great for CJ's traveling, especially when he would be making the trek up the mountain with Gina. Soon she would be there and so would the baby. It just seemed like answered prayer. CJ also spoke with his Mom. They decided that the four of them would celebrate Christmas when they all got together in the summer. After some time of exchanging facts and feelings they all ran out of things to say.

CJ's folks asked that Sheridan be given their regards and prayers for his total recovery. With love and good-byes the phone call was ended. Talking with them had been uplifting and maybe a little tear provoking also. They both missed CJ's parents, but they also loved Raven Hill. Christmas was coming to Raven Hill this year and there would be some celebration. It had been a long time since a tree was brought into the house. Sheridan was funny about killing a tree, unless you were going to use it for income, or heat.

The next day after all the chores and breakfast dishes were cleaned and put away, CJ and Lynn started to make some tree decorations out of odds and ends around the cabin that they saved. Lynn brought out some pine cones, ribbon, and aluminum foil along with some yarn and small sticks, things she had been collecting. All of their Christmas decorations were packed away in their garage which was attached to the house they were renting out.

Sheridan watched as CJ whittled small animals from kindling wood. Lynn was making stick and yarn decorations as she was shown when she was a child. It would be important for Gina to see these on the tree when she came. Lynn went on to make stars with the aluminum foil. The bright colored red and green ribbon would be used to hold the decorations on the small tree that CJ would cut from the back yard. Sheridan watched intently as the two made fancies for the tree he knew would be felled for the festivities.

He spoke to CJ, who sat whittling a set of dogs that represented Donnie's blue tick hounds, and slowly told him that if he went into the small closet where his family's personal items were, that there were a few Christmas decorations his wife and kids had made. Lynn thanked Sheridan for wanting to share his beloved items. CJ scouted around in the closet until he came across a small box marked "Christmas." He handed it to Lynn who had stayed outside the small room waiting to assist him. She took the box over to the sofa next to Pa's chair, dusted off the top and looked inside.

CJ had closed the closet door and headed over to the sofa to see the contents. The items were small and well wrapped. Most of the protection around the decorations were small pieces of material. There were whittled fruits, animals, birds, and even fish. Sheridan picked up a couple of the wooden objects and smiled lovingly. Then Lynn unwrapped beautiful crocheted snowflakes his wife had made. They were in wonderful condition and so ornate. Sheridan reached out to touch one. He then slowly grabbed his walker and made himself rise up and head toward his bedroom. CJ asked if he was alright. Pa answered he was going to go read a little, and he was fine. Donnie and his Dad showed up a few minutes later just as CJ was finishing up the details on the dogs he had whittled. They sure did look like Donnie's hunting buddies.

The snow on the mountain trail was still no problem for traveling. Donnie's pick-up walked right up the side of the mountain with no spinning at all. The two men knocked and walked into the cabin smiling. The first thing Donnie's Pa said was he could not believe the small amount of snow up here on Raven Hill.

"We might have more than you do down below, but not much more."

He then headed down the hall to talk with Sheridan. Lynn stoked up the stove and put on a fresh pot of coffee for the men.

"Well," said Donnie, "with Christmas coming I figured you two would want to put up a tree. I think it might be a good thing for Sheridan, too. It's been years since he even thought about holidays. Pa and I tried to make it up on holidays, with a small gift of a roasted piece of venison or rabbit that we could share with him and he would not be alone. He's been failing since his family has passed. I guess he was really hanging on until he was sure you would take over Raven Hill and love it as much as he does. I got to admit he's doing pretty good. Well, with that being said, let's go chop down a tree for the holy day."

Lynn said, "Go ahead, I'll work on lunch and coffee. The two Pas are having a nice chat, so go ahead and chop. Just be careful guys, watch out for those bears."

Donnie laughed and told Lynn he saw one as they were driving up the mountain. "We'll be fine, it was on the other side of the hill scouting for berries and roots."

Lynn whipped up some pork roll sandwiches with coleslaw and three bean salad. She had been baking cookies for the last few nights so she put out a plate of homemade cookies for dessert. She was setting the table when the two guys entered the cabin.

"Where do you want it, Lynn?" asked CJ.

"I think in the corner farthest from the fireplace."

Donnie moved some furniture around with Lynn's approval. Then the two of them brought in a small tree about 5 ft high and beautifully filled out.

It fit in the corner perfectly. The tree was in a bucket, so it could be easily watered and whatever they used to anchor the tree did a good job.

"There you go. Tomorrow after the boughs drop you will be able to decorate it."

Lynn was thrilled. "OK, great. Wash up and I'll feed you all some lunch."

The cabin was filled with love and friendship. Sheridan and Pa decided they would eat together in Sheridan's room. Donnie took a tray filled with food into them and CJ followed with hot coffee from the pot and some cookies.

When they returned from the bedroom, Lynn had prepared plates for the three of them. Everyone took their time eating and talking. The sandwiches were good and so were the salads but the cookies made Lynn shine. The men loved her cookies and her, too. They enjoyed each others company until late in the afternoon. Lynn offered to make some supper for them all, but the two men decided that they should be going home. Snow wasn't a problem but night would be coming on soon and the trek down the mountain could be tricky with its ruts and snow patches.

The men left and Sheridan watched until they were out of sight. CJ got started with Sheridan's therapy while Lynn started to put some supper together for them. Sheridan told CJ how he liked seeing Donnie and his Pa. He said that Donnie's Pa and him were friends for years. He thought that maybe Donnie's Pa was the last of his friends, at least the last that came to see him. CJ agreed that they were good people.

By suppertime the next day the Christmas tree was decorated with all the little collection of homemade beauties. The tree was beyond beautiful. Lynn made a large, silver foil star that CJ attached to the very top of the tree and it would sparkle and shine, especially when the fire danced in the fireplace. Sheridan was mesmerized by its splendor. The cabin was a home again, not just a place to abide. Everything was pretty much in the same place it always was and it was clean and smelling fresh with life.

Their Christmas was quiet, but very enjoyable. On the trips to the hospital and grocery store, CJ and Lynn had bought gifts for each other and Sheridan. The baby was not even here yet, but still there were gifts under the tree waiting to be opened. Sheridan went through his belongings and found a solid chrome whistle that he cleaned and polished until it glistened. He got a piece of red ribbon from Lynn and he hung it on the tree for the new baby. Whistles are very important when you live in the woods. They can summon you help or allow you to be found if you get lost. It had been in the family for a long time and each of his children had owned it when they were young. Now it would be passed down to his adopted grandchild with love and safety in mind.

A few days passed and as they were finishing up Sheridan's exercises Lynn's cell phone rang. Lo and behold it was Gina calling her from Romania assuring her that she would be seeing her on the second of January. They talked for a short time and then CJ spoke with her so they could coordinate her arrival time at the airport. It was going to be about an hour ride from the airport to Serpentine Gulch. She would have the driver call when they were about 20 minutes away. That would give CJ time to make it to the bottom of the mountain and meet her.

Everything was fine on her end, and she was hardly able to wait. Gina talked again with Lynn. She wanted to know how her pregnancy was doing.

Lynn assured Gina she was fine and ready to deliver. She also told Gina she thought it might be sooner then they all thought. The conversation ended and the anticipation grew stronger. Lynn could hardly wait. It had been a long time and she knew Gina must have changed some, but so had Lynn. Lynn knew Gina was not a stranger to the USA, she or some of her relatives.

Life between the two countries was still very different. The part of Romania that Gina came from was very poor and it was hard to eke out a living. The USA was rich and abundant with everything you could need or want. Lynn was sorry Gina's family was never able to move here and live. Lynn was explaining to Sheridan her relationship to Gina.

CJ decided he would take a walk outside and work on chopping some more wood while Sheridan and Lynn passed time. Sheridan listened to Lynn as she spoke and soon realized that Gina was not really related to Lynn by blood but by their friendship to each others family. Lynn agreed that it was like that.

She asked if Sheridan had any pictures of his family that he would let her see. He said there was a family album in the closet. Lynn retrieved the album which she brought to Sheridan's table. She pulled up a chair and opened the cover. There was his immediate family black and whites, some of which were even brown from age. Each one had been marked with a name and date and activity on the back of it. Many of them no longer were stuck to the picture holders. They covered relatives, pets, and a few friends. Lynn really enjoyed this trip down memory lane with Sheridan. It also gave her a chance to ask questions about the different people she was seeing.

Sheridan spoke about the heartaches of losing his children and the way each one's passing had robbed life from him and his wife. It was really hard to bury his mate, he said. They had been through so much and still loved each other without question. As he spoke, Lynn continued to flip through the pages. As she neared the end of the album, she came to several pages of tintypes. Sheridan said those people were long gone, most of the pictures were of distant family and their friends, homes, and pets. Then came a section of furniture drawings from days gone by up to maybe 10-15 years ago.

"We saved all those style drawings, just in case we would need or want to duplicate one of our pieces of furniture. Some of those drawings are from my father's time."

Lynn still had a few pages left to turn. Sheridan was preoccupied with watching out the window and seeing CJ swing the ax as he split logs into small, stove-sized pieces. Next to the back page were two small pictures, one of a young woman and the other of a young man. Under the picture of the young man was written, "Robert Jake, he was a lazy, shiftless fool and an embarrassment to his entire family." Under the woman's picture it said, "The Gypsy demon who's cursed the Bowers name. May she never find peace, she or her messengers."

Lynn studied the pictures for quite a while then decided it best not to ask Sheridan about them. She would talk to CJ later.

January 2 arrived and Gina was on her way from the airport, still the snow had been slight. It was very cold out but not snow covered, which was wonderful. CJ received the phone call from the airport service driver and he was on his way down the mountain to meet Gina and bring her up to Raven Hill. The house,

Lynn, and Sheridan were ready to accommodate her visit. Gina was more than ready to see Raven Hill and its owners. She had heard a lot about this place.

CJ reached the bottom of the mountain trail within minutes of the airport driver and his passenger. The sky surely looked like snow, but there was none in the immediate forecast. The driver and CJ both exited their vehicles about the same time. CJ went to the back door of the airport taxi and opened it. There was an older woman sitting on the seat, with very distinctive looks and lots of jewelry, old gold, family heirlooms. Her hair was tightly pulled back and a scarf tied under her jaw.

"Well, who are you?" she asked.

"I'm CJ, Lynn's husband."

"Oh, so very nice to meet you," she said. "I'm Gina, Lynn's relative."

"Yes, we've been waiting for you to visit with the three of us."

"The three," she said.

"Yes. Sheridan Bowers, who owns Raven Hill, and Lynn and myself, plus in a short time our baby."

"Sheridan you say. Oh, of course I knew he was the owner, but not for long I understand," she said.

CK was not sure what to say so he just escorted her to the SUV while the driver of the taxi helped put the luggage in the back of CJ's vehicle. After being sure Gina was in and comfortable, CJ went to the back of the SUV to tip the driver and thank him. CJ had a 20 dollar bill folded in his hand which he held out for the driver to take.

The driver waved away CJ's hand politely. "You taking her away from me is thanks enough. She is a nosey, bitter, old lady, who should have stayed in Romania. I'm sorry to offend you, but it's the truth. She said she was staying a short time, just to be sure things would finally be the way they should have always been."

CJ just thanked the man again and they both got into their vehicles and left. CJ told Gina how much he and Lynn were looking forward to her visit and help. He surely hoped she could tolerate living up on Raven Hill with little access to stores and people.

"I only need family around, not stores, not strangers," was her reply.

CJ drove on, thinking maybe the taxi driver was right, she was different.

"How is Lynn?" Gina asked.

"Ready to deliver. Tired but happy."

"That's good, that she is happy. The other two things will pass. Sadness and anger live forever."

"Right," said CJ.

They crested the top of the hill and Gina could see all of Raven Hill in its winter glory. She drew her breath in, astonished at the way it looked. She wiped her eyes with her crocheted hanky and under her breath she said, "Yes, now I know."

CJ drove to the front porch and Lynn was at the door waiting and waving. CJ helped Gina out of the SUV and into the house. Lynn hugged Gina and cried. Gina patted Lynn's back and told her things would be fine, she was there to make sure everything and everyone was taken care of. Lynn backed up to show off her baby belly and Gina smiled and started to remove her coat, scarf, and gloves. Sheridan sat quietly by the fireplace.

Lynn said, "Gina, let me introduce you to Sheridan Bowers. His family has owned Raven Hill from its beginning."

"That's quite an accomplishment, Mr. Bowers."

Sheridan said nothing, he just studied her.

"Well, let's have some hot drinks and relax. Gina, you must be exhausted from traveling."

"I am tired, but I want to hear how you are and your future plans."

CJ brought in Gina's luggage and took it to the room she would be using. Then he came out to talk with Sheridan. The two decided they would give Gina and Lynn some space in the kitchen. CJ took two cups of coffee in Sheridan's bedroom, then came back to walk with Pa to his room.

"It's good to see that you are able to walk on your own Mr. Bowers. I heard you had several health problems. Do be careful, as we get older our minds and bodies are not always in sync."

Sheridan stopped and looked at her and said that for Lynn's sake he was glad she was here. Not to worry about him, he knew his home and property like the back of his hand. The Almighty would guide his steps.

Gina shrugged her shoulders and turned back to Lynn. The men did Sheridan's therapy after their coffee break and Lynn and Gina talked for hours at the table. Lynn served up some beef stew for supper with crusty bread and fresh spice cake for dessert.

The men stayed in Sheridan's room to eat also. Lynn served Gina and then bowed her head.

"Excuse me Lynn," said Gina, "but I must go outside before I eat."

Lynn started to tell Gina where the privy was but common sense must have taken her to the back door. Gina finished tying her scarf and turned to Lynn and said, "Please start without me or I will feel bad."

"I'll wait so we can give thanks together."

"Please eat, the baby is hungry, and thanks I can give on my own dear."

Lynn said grace and ate so as not to upset Gina. Gina closed the back door and took a deep breath of the cold air. She then headed for the half moon shed feeling wonderfully at peace. She was proud she was able to make the trip, and see was glad to see Lynn. On the two men she would hold her judgment. There would be ample time to get to know them.

After the dishes were done and the kitchen was cleaned up, everyone decided to go to bed. The women would start to reminisce in the morning after breakfast. Sheridan was already in bed, looking out his window at the sky and moon. He just laid there thinking about the visitor in his cabin and how unique she was. CJ was in bed listening to Lynn rattle on about Gina and their childhood and how close Gina stayed to Lynn over the years even though they were countries away from each other. Lynn continued to talk as CJ drifted off into dreamland.

While Gina was staying with them at Raven Hill, CJ was pretty much in charge of Sheridan's needs except for food and drink. Naturally the women did the clothes and cleaned the cabin. The men and women seemed to always be apart in different rooms of the cabin. They would take their meals together but then split up again. Gina would ask questions and Lynn would gladly answer her in great detail. Lynn told her how all this had come about, how sickly Sheridan was, how wonderful Donnie and his Pa were, and how they had lost their two blue tick hounds to the ravens. How the birds seemed to be attracted to the hospital and then to the helicopter. How they attacked CJ and his friends.

She had called for knowledge from an ornithologist but they said that it was never heard of before and that the birds must have felt threatened to act in such away. They had given her the idea they thought she was losing her mind and taking up their time. Gina said she noticed the black birds in the tree over the graveyard.

"That's where they perch all the time," Lynn said.

Gina tapped her finger to her lips and said, "I wonder why there."

Lynn told her Sheridan said it was a curse from an evil woman who had tried to take advantage of one of his relatives. Gina laughed and squinted her eyes. "Well, maybe later I will take a little walk around outside."

"I'll get CJ to go with you so you don't fall."

"Fall?" said Gina, "I come from Romania. There we get much snow and I walk alone."

Lunch was made by the ladies and after lunch Sheridan and CJ fell asleep in their chairs by the fireplace. Gina convinced Lynn to nap also. She would finish up drying the dishes and would rest also. The cabin was quiet and the dishes were put away. The three owners were sound asleep.

Gina put on her coat, boots, scarf, and gloves, and very quietly exited the backdoor. The air had a nip to it and the day was overcast. Gina took her time wandering around the homestead looking into sheds and generally surveying the grounds. She visited the landing and ended her trek at the gates of the cemetery. All the while she walked she mumbled under her breath words that were not audible. She glanced up at the ravens in the oak tree and then entered the cemetery. With gloved hands she brushed snow off the burial markers and hesitated at each gravesite. The last one she observed was Robert Jakes. There she hesitated, but she also knelt down and lingered.

In the cabin Sheridan had awaked from his nap, and he watched as she had violated his family's resting place with her nosiness. She finally stood up and left the cemetery slowly, but she continued to look back over her shoulder to the graves.

Sheridan carefully and quietly stood up from his chair and with his walker he headed toward his bedroom. He closed his door as Gina opened the rear cabin door and proceeded to take off her outer garments. CJ stirred and Gina announced it was just a short hike from the cabin to the privy. CJ agreed and then wondered were Lynn and Sheridan were.

"Lynn is napping and Sheridan was in his chair by the fireplace when I went out," she said.

"Well, he probably went to his room to read or go through his old family albums. He really misses his family."

"So do I," interjected Gina.

"I'm sure you do," said CJ.

The days passed uneventfully. The women shared cleaning and cooking. Lynn tired very easily, but Gina was truly a ball of energy, her age did not slow her down one bit. She would do it all, cook, clean, wash clothes, and hang them out to dry or freeze. If they froze, she brought them back in and hung them throughout the cabin to dry.

Lynn and CJ welcomed her visit with them. Poor Sheridan for some reason seemed to spend more time in his room sleeping. CJ was concerned about Sheridan and he called Dr Miles, who put his mind at rest by saying it's winter and gloomy out. He's old and recouping from his stroke. Let him rest, as long as he eats and drinks worry not. Well, Sheridan was eating and drinking, but he was not himself. He slept through a lot of therapy sessions and he read very little.

Chapter 15

*I*t was the third week in January. The supper dishes had been cleaned and put away. The sun was almost gone. Sheridan was laying in his bed, feeling as though the life was draining from him. He did not want to alarm CJ by telling him he did not feel well, especially with Lynn being so close to delivery time. He had some good days and then something would happen and he would feel weak and shaky. Sheridan closed his eyes to rest for a minute and in came Gina with his evening snack and milk.

"I really don't want anything more. Please leave and take it with you."

"You must eat to get better, Mr. Bowers. CJ and Lynn will worry if you don't eat."

"Leave it and go, I'll eat later."

"I'll be back in one half hour and it better be gone or I'll tell CJ immediately."

"Go woman and don't argue with me. Out of my room or I'll talk with CJ about you going back to Romania. Now out."

Gina was furious with Sheridan, but she would not let anyone know about the discord between them. Gina shut his door behind her and went to serve a cup of tea to CJ and Lynn in front of the fireplace.

Sheridan did not want food, nor did he want to upset CJ and Lynn. It was barely light out. He forced himself to stand and, with the aid of his walker, he ever so slowly and weakly made his way to the window. With all the strength he could muster he opened the window a crack. First he threw out the snack cake, then he poured the milk on top of it without even trying. It took all the energy he had remaining to close the window and put the glass back in its place. With all of his strength sapped, down he fell, hitting his head on the night stand.

CJ and the women heard the noise and rushed to his room. There he laid on the floor with blood running out of his brow. CJ rushed over and Sheridan reached for him.

"What happened, Pa?" he said.

"My feet got tangled up and I mis-stepped." CJ helped him into bed, realizing how weak Sheridan had become in the past few weeks.

"Are you ok, Sheridan?" asked Lynn.

"I'm fine, Lynn. Please don't worry."

"There is no reason to worry," said Gina. "I have everything here to clean him up and bandage his wound, so please leave me to my work. Take Lynn back to the fireplace and finish your drinks. He'll be fine."

Gina bathed Sheridan's brow with warm water as he laid still. "I'm glad to see you finished your snack, old man. It will help you to rest." She then bandaged his wounded head. "You're lucky I did not have to stitch you up, especially since you're not a drinking man, the pain would have been nasty."

Sheridan opened his eyes and glared at her. There was something evil about her, not caring or kind, not toward him. She picked up the leftover bandage and scissors along with the dirty basin and cloth and turned to leave.

"I'll be right back to collect the snack dishes and tuck you in real good so you don't get up again and fall."

Gina returned and pulled the bedding tightly and placed it under the mattress. "That should keep you put Mr. Bowers." Then she turned around and picked up the saucer and glass from the end table. "Good thing you did not break the glass or saucer."

Sheridan waited until she left and then he struggled to release the bedding that held him captive. He laid looking out the window at the silhouettes of the birds against the dimly lit sky. They were always watching the cabin, or at least it seemed that way.

Morning came and Sheridan awoke with a large goose egg on his brow and a large headache to go with it. CJ came in and helped him to the commode and got him dressed to greet the day.

"I brought your medicine with me and a glass of water, Pa. I thought you might want a little something for the headache you must have, too."

"Thank you," Pa said. "Looks like we will have a little sunshine today."

They both looked out the window and welcomed that thought. Sheridan was up and sitting in his bedroom chair when Lynn walked in with pancakes and sausage along with juice and coffee.

"Here Sheridan, I made one of your favorite breakfasts, I hope it makes you feel better."

Gina stood to the side of the door and listened to the conversation without being seen, then she headed toward the kitchen for a cup of tea. After a light lunch that Lynn put together for them, CJ convinced Sheridan to go to the sitting room for a change of scenery. It was slow walking but he made it to his fireplace chair. Gina offered to clean up his room and change his bedding. Lynn said she'd help, but Gina told her to relax and rest. Lynn went to her own room and wrote in her diary, something she'd started doing the first day she moved to Raven Hill.

Gina changed the bedding and tidied up the room. As she turned to leave the room she saw that something had been spilt on the window. She grabbed a corner of the dirty bedding and was starting to wipe off the glass, when she saw several dead birds lying under the window. There was also the remains of snack cake from the night before.

Gina hissed and said, "The baby will come and he will go. Mountain man or not, he's not going to win."

Gina left the room and excused herself to go to the privy. Sheridan had been talking with CJ and he was feeling a little better and a little stronger. CJ went to find Lynn and see if she was OK. Sheridan peered out the window just in time to see Gina coming around the corner and heading toward his bedroom window. Sheridan at once noticed the dead birds on the ground and realized he was in a fight for his life and maybe all their lives. He had to get stronger. He couldn't tell CJ and especially not Lynn. He could not eat or drink unless CJ or Lynn made it. Who was this woman and why was she plotting his demise? Gina caught sight of Sheridan watching her and she held up the dead raven to show him she knew he knew and this would be a fight to the death. She waved her raven filled hands and her mouth was moving. As Sheridan watched, he knew alright, he knew she was evil and strong.

Sheridan searched his mind for a reason. His thoughts always came back to the curse. How would someone from Romania be a part of his past? He did not know where Romania was or that it existed before CJ took time to show him a map prior to Gina's coming. He had mixed feelings about himself and his family. The Bowers truly liked being cut off from the world and its ugliness. He was glad his children had been sheltered. He totally understood protecting and keeping generations of Bowers faithful and true to themselves and to their beliefs, yet on the other hand he was also unable to relate to all that happened in the world, and all the mislead people and their beliefs. Now it was at his door and once again directly affecting the lives of people he loved. He was sure of one thing, he would not lose one more family member to this Bowers curse. He would reach down deep inside of himself and he would plot and fight this with all that was within him.

Gina left the side of the cabin to dispose of the birds and the snack cake she found. Sheridan continued to watch out the window and think. He could not be fearful, it gave strength to Gina. He must find her weaknesses and her motives. Lynn entered the room with CJ. She asked Sheridan if he would like some company for a while so CJ could restack wood on the porch from the shed. The supply was getting low, and even though there was no chance of snow on such a bright sunny day, it was still very cold and windy outside. Sheridan welcomed her company, he and she both would be safer together. Before sitting down on the sofa Lynn went to the stove and got Sheridan a fresh cup of coffee and herself a hot tea.

"Here you go," she said, as she placed the cup in front of his chair.

"Where is Gina?" he asked in reply.

"She's out on the back porch doing wash and hanging clothes to dry. She thought it was best to take advantage of the sun and wind."

"Lynn, could you make it clearer to me, your relationship to Gina? I did not know that your family was from Romania."

"I'm not from Romania, my folks lived here in the United States. They had friends in Romania, and I can remember being told that I had been there, I guess on visits. Most of it was just a vague memory to me. When I got older and graduated from High School, my mom and dad sent me to Romania to visit with people they were very close to. That's how I finally met those who my folks had given family titles to, such as my Great Aunt Maria, who was very old and in poor health. There I also met and bonded with her daughter Gina, who I adore and love.

"All through the years, even up to the present, she has always written to me faithfully and she has sent me many gifts of jewelry, clothes and money. I tried to send them back, but she was very heart broken to think that I thought of them as unwanted trinkets and trash. Through the years I've kept most of the items she has sent, especially the ones that she said had special meaning to her."

Sheridan asked what Gina did for a living when she was a younger woman.

"The same thing she does now," answered Lynn. "She is a well established mid-wife in Romania. That's her title, but she is well versed in the medical field. There's not too much she can't do. Aren't we fortunate that she has that training. She knew how to care for your injury the other night without even thinking twice. She certainly is gifted, it appears."

"I bet you wish you and she were related after all the wonderful past times the two of you have enjoyed."

Lynn smiled and said it did not matter if they shared a bloodline, they were bonded by fate. CJ returned from his wood chopping and he resupplied the wood boxes on the porch and in the kitchen. Lynn asked if he thought he might be overfilling the boxes some. CJ said no, had she looked outside recently. Lynn and Sheridan both peered out the window and saw the snow coming down and covering everything like a thick blanket. Neither of them could believe their eyes.

Where did the sun go so fast and when did the wind cease to blow? CJ announced that the wood was in good shape now and he was going to help Gina with the clothes. He said he caught sight of her taking down clothes on his last trip to the porch. He headed toward the back door. Sheridan and Lynn were riveted to the window watching the snow fall.

CJ was getting ready to exit the back door when he saw Gina removing the last couple of articles from the line. He was awestruck to see several ravens perched on the clothes line as well as the one perched on her shoulder. His first thought was to yell to her to run, but then he realized that she was entertaining them. The raven on her shoulder saw CJ and cawed out loud. Gina swung around and yelled for CJ help from the bird attack upon her. The birds flew away and Gina realized that maybe she did not fool CJ. She faked fearful crying, and went past him into the cabin to get mercy from Lynn. CJ gathered up the clothes and took them into the cabin, along with a basketful that was dried earlier.

Inside he was torn about demanding an answer from Gina about why she was entertaining the killer birds. He knew what he saw and she was at peace with them. His other thought was Lynn's and Sheridan's safety. He must talk with Pa and it must be done secretly. CJ could hear Gina crying in Lynn's bedroom, and he could hear the compassion in Lynn's voice.

He went to the chair that Sheridan was sitting in and Sheridan could see the confusion in CJ's eyes. Sheridan reached out and took his hand and he could feel it shake with fear and anger.

"Pa, we must talk, it's about Gina."

"Shh," said Sheridan with his finger to his lips. "She is a witch with strong beliefs in herself and her mission. We must say nothing, but act concerned for her safety. I, too, have seen her, and she is aware I know. Keep an eye on our food and drink."

"Lynn, Pa, what about Lynn?"

"She is fine and coveted by Gina. Fear not for her, it's us she wants to destroy."

"Why?"

"I don't know yet, be alert."

Lynn was able to calm down Gina and CJ played along by going to the bedroom and demanded that she tell him she was alright.

"I'll get my gun from the mantle and I'll shoot the ones in the cemetery tree."

"No, no," said Gina, "it's far too nasty outside, you'll catch your death."

CJ started to put on his coat on, when he heard Gina yell up the hall that they were gone.

"Just as you said, CJ, they left when the snow came."

Lynn agreed with Gina that it was CJ who said they would leave when snow came and snow was really coming down and piling up. Sheridan and CJ both looked toward the cemetery and there were no black images anywhere on the tree. Sheridan placed his hand over his forehead and pondered what he had seen. Lynn had started a large pot of chicken vegetable soup early that morning, so the men knew they could eat. The stove was always in plain view, so observing who was cooking was easy. Lynn left Gina to rest in her own room, while she prepared biscuits to go with the soup.

The cabin was quiet and warm and the soup smell had danced its way through the entire place. Sheridan and CJ ate and drank well, the biscuits with jam on them was dessert enough for both of them. Lynn ate with Gina in Gina's room. Later Gina came out and made tea for both of them and returned to her bedroom to interact with Lynn. CJ cleaned up the dishes and kitchen and took account of the food in the refrigerator. Pa and he had coffee and watched the wood in the fireplace burn. CJ went out to get a couple of logs for the night and announced that the snow had pretty well stopped but nothing would be moving for a few days. As he spoke he hoped that meant the baby would not choose to enter the world until next week as planned.

While the two men sat in front of the fireplace, Lynn went into Sheridan's room and removed his family album. She wanted to show Gina Sheridan's family and she also promised Gina that she would show her a picture of the two people in the back of the book who were removed from the Bowers clan. Lynn slowly went from page to page showing and explaining to Gina who was who according to Sheridan. Gina watched and listened but she really wanted to see the back page, the one with the two pictures that were apart from the rest of the family.

When they came to the tin types things became a little more interesting to Gina. She saw Sheridan's mother, father, uncles' and aunts' images. Gina remarked how strong the family resemblance was through the ages. Then finally the last page came into view. Gina grabbed up the book and stared at the pictures. She was riveted to the man's and woman's faces. Lynn thought it to be slightly strange that Gina would show so much interest in the pictures. Finally Gina offered to return the book to Sheridan's room.

"It's his personal property and we must respect that," said Gina on her way out the door.

Lynn liked the way Gina was always direct and to the point about things and like Lynn she enjoyed being in control of a situation. Lynn liked everything about Gina. She especially liked being important to her. Gina came back in with another cup of tea for Lynn.

"I don't think I can hold anymore," said Lynn.

Gina stretched out her hand with the cup in it and said, "You must have a lot of fluids, you're drinking for two. Your body will need lots of nourishment so you can feed your little one when she comes."

"She, you said 'she' Gina."

"Well, it's just a guess. I'm probably wrong. We'll see."

Gina stayed in her room and Lynn went to the sitting room to be with Sheridan and CJ. She sat down on the sofa next to CJ and watched the wood burn. After a time Sheridan decided he was tired and he wanted rest.

"I can make it to my room, CJ, and prepare myself for sleep. I feel much better and stronger. It's Lynn's good cooking I'm sure."

"Will you be able to get yourself up in the morning?" asked CJ.

Lynn listened for Sheridan's answer and he said, "Yes, I will be fine my son."

Down the hall he went. CJ could hear his door shut and lock.

"What was that about, CJ?"

"Sheridan is self conscious about being caught disrobed or using the commode so he decided to lock his door at night."

"What if he falls or calls out to you for help.

275

"I will be able to open the door, I know how to bypass the locking mechanism."

Lynn settled back to watch the fire burn. Once she was fully relaxed, she felt the first sharp pain in her abdomen. Gas, she thought to herself, and maybe over indulgence in liquids, too. She decided to go to the privy one last time before turning in. CJ and she bundled up and headed out the back door. CJ walked in front of her to stomp down the fresh snow and she followed close behind him. The hike back was easier and Lynn was glad to get back inside. She hung up her outside coverings and started down the hall.

She stopped at Gina's open door to say good night when she suddenly bent over in pain. CJ and Gina rushed to her aid. Gina realized with great concern that she was going to have a baby and there was no way to get outside help. Gina told CJ to get Lynn into bed. Gina covered the bedding with a large rubber sheet that she produced from her luggage and then she placed a flannel sheet over that. CJ was really worried, he also knew there was no way of getting any outside help. The wind was picking up and the helicopter would not fly in blowing snow. Gina could sense the fear in both CJ and Lynn.

"I am here and everything is under control. Women in Romania call on me for their deliveries and there are never others to help. The babies come as they always did and that's life. It will be a long night and tomorrow we will have grown by one more member."

Gina was talking directly to Lynn. Sheridan had come to his bedroom door to see what the commotion was. CJ alerted him to the fact Lynn was in labor. Sheridan backed into his room and shut the door. Labor was not his skill and he did believe Gina would do the very best she could for Lynn and the little one to come. Gina told CJ it would be best for him to rest in the sitting room, it would probably be a long night. After delivery tomorrow she, Gina, would need to rest and CJ would have to take care of Lynn, as well as the baby and Sheridan.

"I will be by Lynn's side all night and I will call you just before birth occurs."

"I love you, CJ," said Lynn. "Rest, I'm in good hands and I don't want you to see me in labor."

CJ told Gina to leave the door open and he would go to the sitting room. He hurried to the sofa by the fireplace where he reached into his pocket and took out his cell phone. He punched in Dr. Adams' emergency phone number but his call could not be completed because of the weather conditions. He told himself not to worry, even Dr. Adams thought Gina was able to handle delivery if necessary. Sheridan and CJ were both seeking divine help for Lynn and the baby.

Hours had passed and CJ was coffee'd out and exhausted, no matter how much caffeine was in him. He had checked on Lynn about 12 o'clock. She was working with her pains and trying to rest when she could. Gina was right that CJ's uneasiness was obvious to Lynn and it made her labor harder.

It was now 4 o'clock and he sat down after stoking the fireplace and drifted off to sleep. He was awakened at 6:30 by the sound of Lynn moaning loudly, followed by the sound of a new voice crying. He bolted from the sofa to the bedroom just as Gina was swaddling the baby in a warm, clean blanket, and handing the little stranger to Lynn. Lynn cried and cooed and the baby quieted right down. CJ went to the side of the bed and watched Lynn hug their child with such love in her eyes.

"It's a girl, CJ, and she's perfect."

"She even has my dark hair and jaw line. Maybe your nose and definitely your lungs."

She was beautiful and fair with dark hair and eyes, just like her mother.

"Where did you get that blanket from, that the baby's wrapped in?"

"Gina gave it to us. It's got her family's crest on it."

"Funny considering all that's gone on up here, huh?"

There it was, a large black raven, carrying a small tree in its mouth. The chill ran down CJ's spine but he just smiled at his two girls. Sheridan was up and dressed and he knocked on the open door to see the baby.

Lynn said, "Here comes Great Pa, sweet heart," referring to the baby.

Sheridan smiled and went closer to the bed to see the two girls. He saw the blanket and the blood drained from his face .CJ got him a chair and he sat and looked. Gina came around the corner and announced that mother and baby need rest.

"Get that old man out of here, and you, too, CJ."

Lynn said, "Easy, Gina, CJ is a daddy now and Sheridan is a Great Pa."

"Great Pa," Gina barked. "He is no relative, he is a Bowers, not a Barbu. Get him out of here."

CJ escorted Sheridan to the kitchen for some breakfast and coffee.

"I'll be out to cook very soon," said Gina.

"No, no, don't worry," said CJ. "I can cook for Great Pa and myself. "You get some sleep, I can take over now."

CJ was making bacon and eggs when Gina came down the hall and told him the two girls were sound asleep and she was going to rest for awhile.

"Knock on my door if you need me. Do not just barge in."

Gina looked at them both very sternly and headed toward her room. Once inside she sat on the bed and basked in the fact that she'd delivered Lynn's baby. It was just working out so well and so easily from her point of view. Gina stood up and unlatched her small luggage bag, reaching in to the far left corner. She retrieved two small pictures, the ones that were in Sheridan's album originally, of Robert Jake and the unknown woman. Gina sat gazing intently at the two pictures. She then returned them to her luggage and latched the lock tightly.

"Curse," she said, "I'll show Sheridan and his beloved "son" more than a curse. I will remove the most precious person from each of them."

Gina then retired for some much needed rest. She was exhausted and she was not getting any younger. Lynn was so thankful to Gina for saving her and her baby girl. What would Lynn do without her?

Lynn was a natural mother, she had no problem nurturing and nursing her little one.

CJ fed Sheridan and then Sheridan retreated to his chair by the fireplace to look out the windows and read. CJ took some food and drink into Lynn. She was just waking up as he entered the room. He could see the motherly glow in her eyes.

The little girl was sleeping peacefully in the bed next to her Mom. CJ was so very proud of Lynn and awe struck by the baby. He repeated his love and pride to Lynn over and over. Lynn reminded him that Gina should get some credit too, after all, without her things could have gone very ugly. CJ admitted he was glad she was capable of midwifing. Lynn ate some breakfast and drank her tea and juice.

He thought it best to let her rest. He kissed them both and left the room.

Sitting down by Pa, CJ chuckled to himself about Gina not wanting to hear that Pa Bowers would be the baby's official Great Pa. He decided to let Pa in on his thoughts.

"What did she say about that, CJ?"

"She said you could not be the little one's Great Pa because you were a Bowers, not a Barbu."

"What is a Barbu, CJ?"

"I don't know, but it really upset the old girl."

They both laughed quietly, but they were still puzzled on that Barbu thing.

Chapter 16

Days and weeks passed and Lynn and the baby both got stronger and the bonding was great. Gina had worked hard at manipulating to put a wall between Lynn and CJ. She also convinced Lynn that it was best to keep the baby girl away from Sheridan, after all he was sickly and probably a walking germ bag. As far as CJ went, Gina told Lynn that he had made it very clear that he did not like her at all. Supposedly he also told Gina that he would have her shipped out if she said anything to Lynn about their conversations.

Lynn could not believe what Gina was telling her. CJ was not like that. Gina really would spread on the "poor misunderstood me" routine when she spoke to Lynn about CJ and Sheridan. On the other side of her scheme, she would do whatever she could to keep Lynn and CJ apart. He was sleeping on the sofa nights, because Gina told him it was too hard for Lynn and the baby to move with him there. Gina told Lynn that many times when men become fathers they no longer care about the mates. They find themselves looking at their wives as human cows.

With all this going on, the tension in the cabin was starting to rear its ugly head. CJ, Sheridan, Lynn, and Gina were all sniping at each other. Gina was loving it. The wall was going up and division would be much easier now.

After the weather finally cleared and cell phone service was restored, Dr. Adams was notified of the birth of the baby and an appointment was made to see both Lynn and the baby. The mountain trail would be passable and CJ would drive Lynn to town. They would be gone for a quite awhile, since they also needed to do some food shopping.

Gina was waiting patiently for that day. She would gladly take care of Great Pa. CJ was also thinking about that day, so he secretly made plans with Donnie and his Pa to stay at Raven Hill until CJ and Lynn got back home. He had called Donnie on his cell phone from the wood shed. He filled him in on what had happened since Gina had arrived. He wanted to be certain that under no circumstances could Sheridan be left alone with her.

The appointment was two days away. Donnie was bringing some venison and veggies with them for lunch. They would just pop in before CJ and Lynn left. They both could not wait to see little Miss Rolley.

The four adults and baby were in the sitting room after supper. Sheridan had gotten considerably stronger and his speech had improved also. CJ threw a log on the fire and then he sat back down on the open sofa. Gina made it a point to stay close to Lynn's side. Gina would praise Lynn about everything she did and said. She would take Lynn's side on all matters concerning the baby or Lynn. CJ was left out of all their conversations and decisions.

"When are we going to agree on a name for the baby?" asked CJ.

"I have chosen a beautiful name for her. It's Gina Marie."

CJ's mouth dropped. "Do I have any input on this?"

"Why, don't you like it? I love Gina and she brought the baby into this world safe and sound, and the name Marie I promised my mother I would use as a middle name if I had a girl."

CJ was afraid of upsetting Lynn, things were rocky between them. Gina gloated on the name. Sheridan watched and observed Gina's body language as CJ and Lynn spoke. Thoughts went off in his head. He stood up grabbed his walker and started toward his bedroom. Once inside his room he got the family album and flipped to the back pages -- the pictures were gone. Where could they be?

He searched around the area that the album was in to no avail. He knew Gina had them and he was now putting things together in his mind. No one would ever believe what was happening.

CJ was still trying to have his baby girl's name changed before it was officially noted on paper at the doctor's office in two days. Lynn heard him out and then she and Gina headed down the hall to Lynn's room. Lynn was turning cold and indifferent to CJ. She did not even like him to hold the baby, and she would not let Sheridan get any closer than 3 feet.

Feathers in the Blood

The day came for the trip to the doctor's. Lynn wanted CJ to stay with Sheridan and she and Gina would go. Gina reminded her that she should not drive until the doctor okayed it so Lynn agreed on Gina's staying at Raven Hill with Sheridan.

CJ took his time banking the fireplace and the kitchen stove. Just at the last minute Donnie and his Pa knocked on the door with black kettle in hand. Sheridan smiled real big and Gina's face twisted, especially when she heard they would be staying all day.

CJ said, "This will workout real well for you Gina, you can rest and relax. The guys know how to take care of Sheridan. They're good friends."

Lynn was standing by CJ with baby in arms and he was in the process of picking up the diaper bag when Gina tried to hand Lynn a final cup of tea.

"Drink this dear, it will keep you warm on the way to town."

Lynn said she was floating from so much tea so she declined, but Gina insisted. It was the last in the pot, and it was at room temperature. Lynn reached for the cup just as CJ realized if Gina could poison Sheridan, she could drug Lynn and confuse her thinking. He turned quickly enough to catch the cup in Gina's hand and send it flying. The tea went everywhere. He apologized but Gina was furious with him. She called him a clumsy, useless ass. Those words laid heavy on Lynn, and the others stopped and stared at Gina. She started to pick up the broken cup as Lynn moved toward the front door by CJ. Sheridan smiled at them and bid them a safe journey.

The two of them were able to talk on the way to the doctor's. Lynn seemed to be more herself the further they rode. They talked over the baby's name and Lynn did remember the first name that was chosen by them and it was a lovely name. She'd promised her mother she would use Marie and then there was Gina who she had such a close bond with. They continued to talk things over while they rode. CJ reminded Lynn of how much he loved her and how beautiful she and the baby were.

His cell phone rang and he gave it to Lynn. He knew from looking at the caller ID that it was his Mom and Dad calling. Lynn talked and bragged about the baby to them. She asked CJ's Mom what her middle name was. Lynn did not want to hang up, she wanted to be with CJ 's Mom, just for awhile she thought.

CJ stopped for gas and Lynn reached into the diaper bag to retrieve a thermos bottle full of tea that Gina insisted that Lynn drink on the road.

"What is that, Lynn?"

"Hot tea. Gina made me promise to drink to and from town."

"Why?" said CJ.

"It's a tonic for me. It's supposed to build up my blood and make me stronger. The truth is, CJ, that for quite awhile I have not felt like myself. Gina said it was the pregnancy and delivery. That's why so much tea."

Lynn started to twist the cap off, when CJ asked her to wait until the doctor gave her a check-up before she drank the tea. Lynn agreed, she said she was really getting tired of it.

The baby and Lynn were examined at the hospital. Dr. Adams and Lynn spoke about how Gina delivered the baby and how Gina would make pots of her special tea for Lynn to drink.

"The tea is building me back up," said Lynn to Dr. Adams.

"Well, that's not what your lab work says. It says you are extremely low in several areas, especially iron. I'm going to insist that you stop drinking that special tea and you start taking these vitamin and mineral tablets daily along with these iron tablets. Drink regular tea if you want. I think you will feel better and think more clearly and recuperate a lot faster. Nothing against you friend Gina, but old mid-wives have old world herbal remedies that aren't always the best."

Gina received a shot of B12 and she took a vitamin from the doctor.

"Now, about this little girl's name. What will it be?"

CJ looked at Lynn and remained quiet. She looked down at her pride and joy and answered, "We will name her Lori Ann, the name we first agreed on. We both just liked the name Lori, and Ann is CJ's mother's middle name, and we both love her, too. My mother wanted me to promise if I had a girl her middle name would be Marie. I'm tired of that name, every woman as far back as I know about in my family carried the name Marie in her name."

"Why?" asked Dr Adams.

"I'm not sure, but it was supposed to have kept power in the bloodline. I never really understood old myths. This will be the first girl on my side not to carry the name Marie."

"I see your name on your chart, and it is Lynn Marie Rolley."

The doctor gave them the necessary forms made out with her name and title on it. Now they would send in the forms to the state and Lori Ann would be officially their little girl's name.

After the appointment, CJ and Lynn stopped for a bite to eat and then they continued on to the grocery store for much needed items. CJ offered to do the shopping. Lynn had written down everything they would need or want. She agreed that she would nurse Lori and rest while CJ shopped. Lynn had a spare blanket in case she got cold and the keys were in the ignition.

CJ was feeling good and he did not mind at all shopping. He could see a change in Lynn already. With the tea leaving her body and the injection and pill the doctor gave her working, she was like her old self. She was getting back the ability to control her feelings. Lynn fed the baby and then closed her eyes to rest.

The next thing she knew was the sound of the back door closing and CJ climbing into the SUV. On the way home CJ told Lynn about several things that had happened since Gina was in control of the cabin.

"It's almost like she wants you to herself. She is trying hard to build a wall around you and the baby. I'm not to sleep with you and Sheridan is a walking virus according to her."

Lynn could not believe her ears but she did know things were uneasy.

"Gina can be a little strange at times and her ideas are sometimes unusual, but I don't think she would ever hurt us."

"Not you and Lori Ann, but Sheridan and I feel we must watch our backs. She will only be here for another 10 days, do you think we can make it until then? Please talk to Sheridan and I will make it a point to let him see and hold Lori. Also, as of tonight I expect to have you in your own bedroom."

CJ leaned over and kissed Lynn. She said she was glad that Donnie and his Pa were with Sheridan while they were in town. CJ agreed with that statement.

Donnie and his Pa were having a good time with Sheridan. They really liked each other's company. The pot of venison was on the stove being kept warm until the men decided to eat. It was into the afternoon and Sheridan asked if his old friend would go to his room with him and help find something he mislaid. Donnie decided to walk outside and get some air and pick up a few more logs from the wood shed for the fireplace and stove.

Gina could hear Sheridan talking with the old coot in his room and she saw Donnie out by the wood shed. She quietly went to her room were she was plotting and scheming. She hurried to the stove, lifted the pot lid, and dropped in a small packet of powder. Then she hurried back to her room to wait for Lynn's return and to hear her announce the baby's name -- Gina Marie. She had waited and planned her whole life for this visit. It was soon to be as it should have been many, many years ago.

Sheridan and his two friends decided to eat before Lynn and CJ got home. Donnie fixed plates for all three of them. He was serving the old men, when Gina came down the hall and offered to help.

"No, thank you, but I'll carve some venison off for you."

"I would not eat that if it was the last thing here."

Donnie could not believe how her moods changed so quickly and how bitter she could be.

"Go sit down and eat."

Donnie walked away and under her breath, she said, "Enjoy it, it's the last time you will all dine together."

The men ate. Donnie and his Pa were good eaters, but Sheridan filled up easily. Donnie and his dad usually ate one large meal a day and it was in the afternoon. Sheridan was given food all day long, so his appetite was light no matter how good that venison was. Sheridan watched as his two protectors fell asleep on the sofas. He called to them, but they would not stir. He arose from his chair and shook each one, but still no response.

Gina watched from the kitchen and laughed. "If you don't want me to kill them, old man, then go to your room so we can talk."

Sheridan's heart pounded in his chest, but he would do anything not to see his dear friends injured. He knew they ate a large meal that she had somehow touched. He also knew he was sleepy himself as he rambled down to his room with Gina behind him, telling him today he would meet his beloved family, and tomorrow he would be just another cemetery marker for the ravens to sit above and laugh.

"Hurry," she said as she pushed him. "Lynn and your beloved CJ will be home soon."

She pushed him unto the bed, then she tied him to the bed frame so he could not move at all. She reached into her pocket and brought out a syringe of potassium.

"This is your ticket out, old man Bowers. When they find you later tonight they will think you had a heart attack, and no one will question it. I'll say you asked me to help you to bed. You were not feeling well and those two fools out there fell asleep and you did not want them disturbed. You see, I am the curse. I am Lynn's mother, not just a friend. Her adoptive mother was my younger sister. My mother, Marie Barbu, was the woman who your precious relative, Robert Jakes, courted and got pregnant, then his family ran her off the property. She returned to Romania and had me, Gina Marie Barbu. I in turn conceived a lovely girl who is CJ's wife, Lynn Marie Celan, which was my sister's married name.

"We planned and staged her whole life. We had to weaken the last remaining Bowers and somehow take ownership of Raven Hill. It was to be my mother's after poor Robert Jake met his demise, but fate killed him too soon. We now knew how much you loved CJ and the ravens kept me informed of all that went on here. Lynn has always been devoted to me, why not, she's my little girl.

"Mother lived to see the beginning of Lynn and CJ's courtship and I promised to carry on until the Bowers lost everything to the Barbus. A little gypsy witchcraft didn't hurt. Yes, we Barbus are gypsies from Romania. Mother was going to make a place for her family here in the USA by marrying into stability. You high and mighty Bible toting Bowers looked down your nose at the great Sophia Marie Barbu, so she laid a life long curse on anything with the Bowers name on it.

"You will be gone, then next I'll have something nasty and fatal happen to CJ, then Lynn will lean totally on my judgment about her future and the future of my grand-daughter, Gina Marie Rolley. I will introduce her to male friends from Romania and she will marry and Raven Hill will come to its rightful owners, the Barbus. Then I will confess my shame of having Lynn out of wedlock. I will say I did not think myself worthy of her and that I was so poor and my sister loved her as much as I did and I win."

Sheridan could hear and see the ravens in the oak tree screaming and jumping on the branches.

"Look, my messengers are so happy that this will soon be over, after all, their families gave of their time and relatives, too. Until the curse ends the ravens will sit and wait."

Gina started to roll up Sheridan's sleeve when she heard and saw the SUV coming down through the yard. She cursed and put the syringe back into her pocket. Sheridan yelled out for help but Gina slapped tape across his face.

"I'll get you later, old man, unless you die from fear first."

She laughed and went out of the room, locking the door behind her. Donnie and his Pa were waking up to Gina's announcing CJ and Lynn were home.

"Where's Sheridan?" they asked.

"He probably went to lay down and rest as you did. He is used to having a nap every afternoon," Gina said.

Lynn and CJ entered the door and Gina broke into smiles and happiness as she reached for the baby girl.

"What did the doctor say?" asked Gina.

"I'm fine and so is the baby."

"Where is Sheridan?" asked CJ.

"He went for a nap after we ate, we were all tired."

Donnie was going to say more when Lynn asked if they would stay for supper.

"No, Pa wants to get home and I'm wiped out myself. That was rib sticking and heavy, I guess that's why we're bushed."

The two men left and Lynn put the baby in bed as CJ made drinks for him and her. Gina followed her from room to room and made a fuss over her and the baby. Gina would make little remarks about CJ being unconcerned about the new little life and his not being of the same caliber as Lynn. Just constant babbling that made Lynn realize that CJ was right, Gina was not the same person that she remembered.

There was this urgency in her voice, and her loving ways toward Lynn were smothering her and it seemed that all Gina had on her mind was a world that existed with Lynn, the baby, and herself. The more the tea and herbs Gina had given her left her body, the more she regained clarity of thought and feelings. Gina saw the change coming on Lynn and headed toward the kitchen to brew her some nice hot tea, then she would make supper while the two of them rested, so she could kill Sheridan before the sun went down.

CJ went to their bedroom to see Lynn, but she had snuggled Lori up to her side to nurse and they both were half asleep. He closed the door and went to the kitchen to stop Gina from annoying Lynn.

"Asleep," she said, "you tired the poor thing out. She wanted this cup of tea. Best I take it to her."

"No," responded CJ, "let her sleep, Gina. Later for the tea." Gina went to her room to think. Things were not going the way she had planned. Sheridan should be dead by now and CJ would be next to see the pearly gates, but her plans were out of sync. Gina caught sight of CJ heading for the wood shed. She watched out her window until she was sure of what to do. She quietly went down the hall to the back door. The sun had been warm enough to melt the snow earlier, but now she had to be careful of her footing. The night was coming on and the run off was refreezing.

She made up her mind to kill CJ first, then go to Sheridan with the upsetting news of his precious CJ's death. While in his room she would inject him and remove his restraints and gag. Now there was none. Poor Lynn would be so heartbroken and confused that dear Gina would stay on and care for her and the curse would be fulfilled and life would be wonderful on Raven Hill once the Barbu family reigned again. Yes, she must act now.

CJ had his arms full of wood and he started toward the cabin. The night air was cold and the wind had picked up. Just as he got half way across the yard Gina summoned the ravens to kill him. They came like a black sheet and they covered him screaming as Gina laughed from the corner of the house. CJ was putting up a good fight but in time the birds would win. Sheridan could see what Gina had done when the ravens first struck CJ from behind. He was helpless and heartbroken. Gina hurried back inside and played innocent.

Lynn, for whatever reason, awoke startled. She picked up Lori and went down the hall, now she was able to hear CJ's cries as he tried to fend off the attack. Gina saw Lynn go to the door with the baby in her arms. Lynn screamed and Gina knew she would have to save face by waving off the birds. Gina pushed in front of Lynn and started yelling and shooing the birds as she made her way down the front steps.

CJ was still very much alive but battered beyond belief. He saw Lynn and fought even harder against the pecking and scratching.

"Take little Gina Marie inside, Lynn," cried Gina.

CJ heard Gina and for some reason yelled, "Her named is Lori Ann Rolley, not Gina Marie."

Gina spun around and as she did her foot hit a small patch of ice on the step and she fell hard. The birds flew off as one. CJ hobbled to her side and announced that she had broken her neck.

CJ made it up the steps and into the house where he dropped into a kitchen chair and cried. He then got up and limped to Sheridan's room, expecting to find him dead. Sheridan could not believe his eyes, CJ was alive. Pretty hurt, but alive. Lynn was on the phone to Donnie. He would get the law and the coroner up there. He and his dad would be there as soon as he made the necessary calls.

CJ and Lynn helped Sheridan out of his ropes and gag. Sheridan held Lori Ann while Lynn patched up CJ. Sheridan told them the whole story as Gina had told him. They told him how she had broken her neck by catching her foot on the step. Sheridan shook his head and said, "The curse is over. Robert Jakes died just that same way at the beginning of the curse and now Gina died ending the curse."

Lights were coming over the crest of the hill. Sheridan still had his family and Raven Hill and his own life.

Epilogue

Years passed and now Lori Ann was about four years old. She was playing outside under Great Pa's watchful eyes. The sun was warm and that summer was beautiful up on the mountain. Sheridan would give Lori room to explore her yard as she played. Right now they were playing peek-a-boo. Lori would run behind a bush in the yard and then back out to see Great Pa and say peek-a-boo.

She ran behind a bush and did not come right out so Sheridan went to see why. He found her petting a raven and saying, "My bird." When Lori saw Sheridan, she laughed and pointed to the tree in the cemetery and the bird took flight and perched on the limb over Robert Jake's grave.

Lori looked at Sheridan and smiled.

Breinigsville, PA USA
01 April 2010

235330BV00001B/1/P

9 781449 075668